ROBERT WELCH was born in 1947 in Cork and was educated there and at Leeds University. He has taught at Leeds University, at University College Cork, and at Ife in Nigeria. He is currently Professor of English at the University of Ulster at Coleraine, County Derry.

OTHER BOOKS BY ROBERT WELCH

CRITICISM

Irish Poetry from Moore to Yeats
A History of Verse Translation from the Irish
Irish Writers and Religion (editor)
The Oxford Companion to Irish Literature (editor)

POETRY

Muskerry
Secret Societies

FICTION

The Kilcolman Notebook
Tearmann (a novel in Irish)

Groundwork

a novel

ROBERT WELCH

THE
BLACKSTAFF
PRESS

BELFAST

First published in 1997 by
The Blackstaff Press Limited
3 Galway Park, Dundonald, Belfast BT16 2AN, Northern Ireland
with the assistance of
The Arts Council of Northern Ireland

Reprinted April 1998, June 1998, July 1998

Typeset by Techniset Typesetters, Newton-le-Willows, Merseyside

Printed in Ireland by ColourBooks Limited

A CIP catalogue record for this book
is available from the British Library

ISBN 0-85640-608-2

for John Pitcher

DRAMATIS PERSONAE

CON CONDON — son of Mary and Jim Condon, gardener, and Cistercian monk

JIM CONDON — driver in Cork and Leeds; marries Mary O'Dwyer; father of Katherine, Sarah, Ann, Con and Tom

KATHERINE CONDON — daughter of Mary and Jim Condon, later married to Tim Harding

MARY CONDON — *see* Mary O'Dwyer

MICHAEL CONDON — son of Mary O'Dwyer and Morgan Holmes

PATSY CONDON — small farmer in nineteenth-century north Cork; later proprietor of a music shop in New York

KATHERINE HARDING — *see* Katherine Condon

ROBERT HARDING — son of Tim and Katherine Harding

TIM HARDING — factory worker; marries Katherine Condon

RANDALL HERBERT — landowner near Cappoquin, County Waterford, father of Nina Holmes

ELLIOTT HOLMES — merchant wholesaler in Cork city, father of Morgan Holmes

MORGAN HOLMES — merchant wholesaler, husband of Nina Holmes and father of Michael Condon

1955

KATHERINE CONDON

He was always there at three on the dot of a Friday. He'd come in, all bustle, from the blue Morris van, carrying under his arm a chicken, perhaps, or a piece of green bacon. He'd be all business, then, full of himself, in his off-white coat that he'd managed, somehow, to keep when he lost the job in the wholesalers. I don't know what it was with those men. He and his brothers always seemed to be the victims of someone. They were maybe just timorous boys, frightened of their shadows.

The conversation was invariably the same: how he'd told so-and-so such-and-such and shut him up good and proper. But,

Jesus help us, it was always far too evident that he'd never come off the best in any altercation. He'd be the one to be silent under any tirade that anyone (and I mean anyone) would launch. But the vehemence of him, when he'd be talking to me, that is, was extraordinary, a facility that he got perhaps from his mother. She was well able to give as good as she got in any situation.

He'd put the chicken down on the blue Formica table with the air of someone depositing a priceless treasure. He'd open up the greaseproof paper with a great show of zealous enthusiasm, then catch the limp breast between finger and thumb and show how well-fleshed the bird was. 'There you are now,' he'd say. 'A fine roast for the Sunday.'

Then he'd take the tea that would be offered and sit at the fire, hunched up a little, shoulders drawn forward, elbows on his knees, as he held the saucer in one hand, lifting the cup with the other. He'd take out the packet of cigarettes – always tens – and never offer one. He'd light up and inhale deeply the blue smoke. The kitchen would fill with the satisfying smell of burnt match and strong tobacco. Sweet Afton.

He was my elder brother Michael and he earned a fragile living selling produce from his van to family and old customers that did not want to let him down when he lost his job. His needs were simple. He never drank: he was a member of the Pioneer Total Abstinence Association and had never taken a drop in his life. He was a saintly and devout man who revered his priests and attended church every Sunday and on all holy days of obligation. He went to confession regularly. He fasted and abstained during Lent, as required. He was not a fanatical crawthumper, but he was a good Catholic who would never cheat anyone out of a penny.

But goodness, which he had plenty of, is its own reward. There was, indeed, something about him that attracted disaster, and he often found himself being left out of things: weddings, get-togethers, and so on. The earnest face, brown and wrinkled and kindly, would sometimes awaken in me feelings of repugnance, annoyance, impatience, which, to be honest, I'd mostly give in to.

The sisters would often gather in my house and we'd spend hours together when Tim would be on evenings – the four-to-twelve shift in Dunlop's – talking about anything and everything. I liked that. The girl from next door, Geraldine, who had the most beautiful lips I've seen on any woman, would come in and do our hair. The kitchen would stink of the mixture she'd use to give us highlights or perms, while we felt good about the fact that we were getting our hair set at next to nothing. But it wasn't really the money saved that drew us all together on those Thursdays once a fortnight, it was the company and the opportunity it gave us to talk about the men in our lives – brothers, sons, fathers, and husbands. It didn't take long for them to become complete objects of derision. Hardly one of those fortnightly Thursdays went by without one of us saying, in a moment of appropriate silence, our motto, slogan, catch phrase: 'There's not a man born yet that's worthy of any woman.' When we said this we believed it completely, though we knew that it was all a lot more complicated than this, and that the fear of men, of their sharp and acrid reality, was a different matter.

We'd often be joined by other friends and neighbours: the gentle Mrs Falvey, who always referred to her husband as 'James', and who served him his dinner at the very polite hour of five in the evening with, in the winter, the fire lit, and on the table, a linen tablecloth and carefully laid cutlery. Or there was the very different Mrs Barrett, from Ballyphehane, who regaled us with the brilliant outrageousness of her speech. 'For Jesus' sake girls,' she'd say, 'we're right fools altogether and we sitting on gold mines.'

Sometimes the sound of laughter in the kitchen would reach such a high pitch that I'd get worried the neighbours might wonder what was going on. We'd get pains in our stomachs from laughing. We'd often stay like that, my sisters and myself, and any other visitors, talking until Tim would come in from work. Then he'd drive them home after his cup of tea.

Mrs Barrett again: 'Batna' (that was her poor husband's name) 'came in the other night, completely and utterly langers. I could hear him coming in the gate, and when the key turned in the door – it took him a long time to find it, like everything else: he can't tell his arse from his elbow nor the pillow from my backside – I took his dinner from the oven, gave the two lousy chops from Byrne's the butcher's to the dog and threw the rest of the dried-out cinders into the fire. He comes in the door, his eyes blinking like butter wouldn't melt in his mouth. He looks down at me – by now I'd sat myself by the fire again enjoying the sizzle off the greasy spuds – and tries to hold himself steady. "Ma," he says, in a kind of whimper. "Ma, I'm sorry. It was that shagger Tynan again, may the devil blind him. I couldn't get away from him. I only called into the Punchbowl for one or two to ease my throat, but there was Tynan on the bar stool, where he'd sat all day, he told me, too rotten with the drink to go to work." As he was saying this I could see he was rolling on his feet. He had one hand out against the table to try to stop himself from falling down, while the other was rooting around in the pocket of his overalls for something. "Look," says he. "Look, Ma. I got you some bull's-eyes, your favourite." "Shag you and your bull's-eyes," I say. With that he staggers over to where I'm sitting to give me a clatter, but misses his footing and stumbles over, knocking his napper off the wooden arm of the sofa. His raised hand bangs against the back so he hurts himself. That'll put paid to his carrying on with himself in the toilet that he thinks I don't know about, the dirty scut, says I to myself. "Are you all right, Batna?" says I, pretending to be all concerned. "Blast you," says he. "Where's my dinner?" "The dog had it hours ago," says I; "the thing was burnt to a cinder. Have yourself a bate of bread and butter. It's fresh and better than you deserve, coming in in this condition." There I am looking at the sorrowful mystery of his long grey face and me thinking to myself what in the name of Jesus and His Blessed Mother am I doing tied to the likes of this article out of nowhere? And me' – and with this Mrs Barrett would lift her thighs off the stool where she was sitting by the fire, and raise her skirt up to her stocking tops – 'with fine fresh hams on me still like a girl of twenty-four.'

Spurred on by Mrs Barrett's or Mrs Field's (another visitor) rowdiness and spunk, we'd all have a go at the men. My brother, the chicken-vendor, was a favourite topic amongst us sisters, for his poverty, his ineffectuality, his totally false bravado, and the miserable assumptions of certainty he'd make.

'What this country needs,' he'd say, 'is a dictator. A Hitler. Now there was a man with the right ideas. Look at the way this country has gone to the dogs. Gone to the dogs. We need a good strong firm hand to take control and sort out all those bastards up in Dublin. Lining their own pockets. I'll scratch you if you scratch me. The way we are now is this: it's not what you know, it's who you know. And that's always been the same in this country and in this city. Every bloody job in the city hall spoken for by somebody for somebody else's son. Golf clubs. That's what you need to have to be in here. And neck. You have to have neck. Brass neck. A dictator, like Hitler, would clean the lot out and put us back on the straight and narrow which we left when we threw the British out. All that's running this country is a crowd of gangsters and nancy boys. Or if they're not that, they're culchies from the back of beyond who don't know what a pair of sheets is, who've never slept on anything better than a sop of hay.'

He'd go on like this, his little wizened face creasing up as he became more and more seized by his anger. Eventually, if we failed to get rid of him, or if he was at a loose end, he'd end up talking about his days at Holmes's, the wholesalers. It was always a mystery to me that a job could mean so much to a man, but that was the time when jobs were plentiful, which they hadn't been when he was starting out, and which they've stopped being again. His description of spring mornings when he'd set out for the store from the new house on Congress Road became so familiar to us as to be tedious; but now I recognise in them the definite shape of hope.

'I'd set off, Kath, first thing; a cooked breakfast under my belt. On the old bike. Still dark in those March mornings, the light just coming up and I'd coast down Murphy's Lane, the Summerhill South. You'd see the big horses there at the corner, from the flour mill or from the City Bakery down past Langford Row. They'd be queued quietly, just the occasional jangle of their harnesses, or a stamp of a big hoof, tasselled with hair at the bottom. They were lined up for the drinking trough, and they'd get their noses in, five or six at a time. They'd drink, long and deep, with their eyes closed behind the leather blinkers. I'll never forget the horses, Kath. You miss them now. But I'd get the smell of them as I cycled past along Douglas Street. There Mr Long the butcher would already be throwing the sawdust on the floor, cheery and happy with his big belly and horn-rimmed specs. "How are you, Michael boy?" he'd say, but he never raised his voice. Always a gentleman.'

So, I thought, Michael, are you. You may go on about those dictators or whatever in Germany but it's only a let-on. You're quiet like the rest of them. Only the women in the family really shouted. And me, too, like the others. No wonder the Condon women have a reputation. But nice as Michael was, he did go on and on.

'I'd cycle along past the pubs of Douglas Street and the crubeen and bacon shops. Coils of black pudding on marble trays in windows; and the tripe in white enamel dishes. There was the slight incline up Red Abbey Street, before dropping down along the bottom of Barrack Street, along French's Quay and over Clarke's Bridge past the courthouse and the Maltings on the river to where Holmes's wholesalers was. I was just out of school then, thirteen years of age, and thought life was full of wonder and surprise. I'd dismount at the big green gate, and look up and admire its solid wood, carefully painted by professionals. No blisters. Like the green paint work on our new front door at home: fresh and new, and neat against the frosted panes in the upper half of the door that ensured a well-lit hallway. Not like the place we'd left in Tuckey Street, where the ceiling timbers were cracked and damp, and where you'd see the jack rats hopping over the gaps by the candlelight as you lay in bed. And the smell of that place in Tuckey Street: a mixture of iron, and piss, and I don't know what. There's a smell that comes when you scrape burnt toast over a dish of water in the sink, and as the black film settles on the water; it's there. Old and sad and wet.

'I was always early. And I remained punctual right up to the day I was sacked. Always a few minutes to spare. I'd park the bike and stroll over to the river wall and look down along the water towards the curve up the Mardyke. A few swans dipping their heads. Like they were praying deep into the water. Light was brimming now, and I'd see the whiteness of the swans very clearly. I'd pray to God then for our mother, and all of you, and that He'd protect me from all harm. And then I'd light a fag as the swans paddled up to say hello to this human thing at the limestone wall.'

1919

MICHAEL CONDON

The boy looked over the wall, and leaning against it with his hip, he fetched from the pocket of his black serge coat a packet of five Woodbines in their thin green and white paper. Lighting up, he blew the smoke out across the cool air rising from the water. Five swans stayed themselves below the wall. One plunged its head deep when the boy threw the match in a soft arc into the river. They turned, in unison, and with, at first, a slow turbulence of their wings, pushed themselves up out of the water until their webbed feet trawled across the river surface. Then, wings fully extended, they began a slow majestic motion of flight as all five lifted off the dark plane of the river.

Steadily their wings thumped the air to create a hollow groaning sound as they climbed into the morning over the trees. The boy watched them sail above the Georgian houses on the North Mall to fly to the west side of Shandon tower.

He looked down at his new boots, thickly swabbed with black Dubbin boot wax. Even the laces he had impregnated with the soft oily stuff. 'It'll preserve them,' his mother had said last night as he sat in the chair just inside the kitchen door, while she cut the bread for his sandwiches. He burnished the leather to a shine while she filled a small cone made of newspaper with tea and sugar and wrapped the whole lot in brown paper, tying the parcel with coarse white string. The lunch was now on the carrying rack of his bike behind the saddle, held in place by the spring of the metal snapper-tray.

Coming down the street, on the river side, was his work-mate and fellow store boy, Tom Mull from Blarney Street. Tom was no more than two or three years his senior, but he was already almost completely bald, save for a monkish fringe that encircled his pate from temple to temple. He disguised his yellow, nude head by wearing a large floppy cap with the front button on the peak kept open, allowing him to pull the whole thing close down over his eyes and ears, giving him an appearance that was half sinister, half comical. Michael liked this boy, for his bald head, funny stance and strangely lumpish gait. He walked as if he was making his way through boggy ground, giving his feet a slight pull up from the ground at each advancing step. This prancing way of walking was made more pronounced by the fact that he always had his trousers tucked inside his socks above his boots, a technique usually adopted by cyclists to keep their trousers clean of grease, but Tom had no bike. His family, Michael knew, were entirely impoverished and needed every penny he could earn. A bicycle was a luxury.

Tom had the keys to the side door of Holmes's and they went in, Michael lifting his bike over the threshold into the dark interior. They unfastened the inner bolts and lifted the restraining levers from their sockets before pulling back the heavy gates along the polished metal running groove set into the concrete. Behind this, the fifty yards or so of mezzanines, with interconnecting walkways and ladders from level to level where the barrels of corned beef and pickled pork were kept, with the bacon in chests in white snows of salt; the boxes of tea and jute bags of coffee beans; the rows upon rows of spices in jars – turmeric, allspice, coriander, chilli; the white sacks of flour, luminous and plump in the dark light; the bags of chicken feed and Indian maize; and the pervasive smell of brown sugar in the heavy, wax-impregnated sacks. At the back were ranged the big walk-in refrigerators with their engines thundering softly, where they held the chickens, turkeys, cooked meats and fresh pork, as well as long flitches of green bacon and smoked bacon encased in muslin and hanging in rows from hooks; and ropes of salami and smoked sausages dangling in different lengths of variegated red.

The two store boys would light the fire in the office, first cleaning out the massive grate, folding up the cinders in sheets of newspaper, carting them round the back and strewing them over the open space where the horses stood as their drays were loaded up with produce to be delivered all over the city. Then sticks and newsprint would be settled into the grate, coals balanced on the carefully spaced kindlings, and the whole thing lit. Mr Holmes liked a good fire going in the office when he arrived; that is, until the end of the month of April. Above the grate was a cast-iron pulley, a blackened kettle hanging from it to boil the water for the office tea. That would be filled from the brass tap round the back, and set to one side in readiness. Mr Holmes also liked his early morning tea first thing.

1919

NINA HOLMES

Nina Holmes came out of her bedroom into the dressing room, where she and her husband had breakfast together every morning at eight thirty. He was sitting at the table, reading the *Cork Examiner*, toast on a plate before him, a small pile of marmalade to one side. He was wearing the light tweed suit he'd bought in Cash's the week before, a green three-piece, the waistcoat cut high, and above it a winged collar and a flowing red tie, its flamboyance curtailed by a small gold pin. He smelt of eau de cologne after his morning bath. Nina sat on the opposite side of the round table with its starched white linen. Morgan Holmes looked at her, setting the paper aside, his blue eyes drawn to the inch or two of cleavage she had deliberately left exposed when she had drawn the crimson silk Chinese gown around her.

'These agonies of transformation,' he said.

'What are you talking about?' she replied, taking a piece of toast, the crusts cut off, from the silver holder. As she pulled it out a small shower of crumbs sprayed onto the tablecloth, to her mild irritation. She took some butter and pressed it onto the side of her plate with the bone-handled knife, which she then stuck back into the pale block in the dish. She looked at the smooth plane the knife had made in the portion she had deposited on her side plate, and at the contour the pressure had left in the softness beneath. A mild fizz of nervous aware-ness spread over the top of her scalp as she became conscious of the attention she was paying to incidentals. It was too often like this. She looked at the prominent eyebrows of her husband, the hairs of which stuck out in a kind of hirsute searching. Did he comb them forward to emphasise their curious elegance? Perhaps he had a special implement for this, picked up in Paris or Belgrade before the war?

'I'm talking about this so-called War of Independence. That's what I'm talking about. If only people could be left in peace. To work in peace and to conduct business. How can we carry on trading with Britain or Europe or America if we're not sure of supplies or if we don't know from one day to the next who's going to be in control? Or if anyone is going to be in control?'

'Well, Morgan,' replied his wife, 'I'm sure Cork will con-tinue to prosper. We have the export trade, after all, and the supplying of the ocean-going ships.'

She poured coffee into the thin cup and smelt the dark savour. Having sweetened it with a half-teaspoon of sugar, she drank it off at once. The bite of the liquid in her throat and chest stimulated her senses and she looked with freshened gaze out the windows and down the long lawn to the river as it slid past the Mardyke, with its colonnade of elm trees, now virtually deserted at this time of the morning.

'Yes, I suppose so,' he replied. 'I know that our trade should remain secure, no matter what; people always need foodstuffs and animal feed and hardware. But it seemed different in my father's time. Things seemed so much more settled.'

Nina thought of her own father, sitting drunk at eleven o'clock in the morning in the drawing room of his house outside Cappoquin, County Waterford, joking with his tenants who had come mixing menace and jollity to say, once again, that this quarter they couldn't quite make the rent payments. Her father, laughingly accepting his own doom. She'd often see him later on a day like that, standing at the window, hands on the sill beneath him, forehead against the grimy pane. He'd turn when he'd see her enter, all anxiety and fuss, pretending to business. When she'd try to speak to him or touch him he'd move swiftly away, nervously pulling at the tabs of his waistcoat, saying he had to do something in the haggard. Property, she knew, was a burden. She dreaded houses, but mostly she feared the open countryside, its unknowable depths. She dreamed of houses constantly.

'I dreamt last night,' she said, 'of this old mansion. All the windows were smashed in and the estate and gardens going to rack and ruin.'

'Oh yes,' he said. 'Another of your nightmares.'

'I tried to find the way out,' she said, 'but couldn't find the door. I could see the garden outside, in the rain, full of old flowers and bushes. Fuchsia gone wild, hydrangeas long and woody and unpruned.'

But he was getting up to leave, pulling the cuffs down from under his coat sleeves, to show the gold emblazoned with the Holmes family crest. Then he was gone and she was left looking at the butter on her side plate, where the knife had made a soft swoop into the yielding yellow deposit, leaving traces of the imperfections along its edge down the tiny wall. She tried to breathe more slowly.

1600

MOUNTJOY

Charles Blount, Lord Mountjoy, had an erection. He was riding down a muddy hill towards the South Gate of Cork with a group of five Irishmen. Spies, advisers, assistants to Her Majesty. He'd been out to consult with spies of the MacCarthys, near Blarney, and was now headed into the town for a council of war. The weather was appalling. Hail drove against him, making him draw up his cheeks in a grimace and furrow his brow, so that his eyes peered through the merest slits. There were dartings of pain caused by the hailstones all over the upper part of his face. From nose to throat was covered by a thick vizard of jute. His throat hurt, and he could smell his own foul breath under the cloth. Every inhalation was an effort and his chest felt punctured with a mosaic of jagged glass. What felt like a spike pushed at him in his gut. But he had an erection.

He was thinking of Penelope Rich, his mistress back in London, how she had sat on the side of the bed in full daylight on their last occasion together, the curtains pulled back to let in the autumn sunshine. He was lying down behind her, so she was between him and the light. Her gold hair was unloosed and was a radiant monstrance above him, while the reddish glow of the sunshine emphasised the auburn and white tintings in its cloudy aureole. Then, unclasping her stays from behind, she turned to him, opening her black eyes wide in pretended mockery. He saw the two dark stars of her breasts. He wished he were back there, in London, out of this driving hail.

He looked at the face of the man beside him, an O'Kelly from the town. He hadn't shaved for days, and the typical Irish moustache debouched over his lower lip to straggle down each side of his slack mouth. O'Kelly rode straight in the saddle, however, and apart from his incessant nibbling at his long moustache, he was still and mostly quiet. He'd sometimes issue long sighs, which plumed out from his face in the cold.

They got to the South Gate. The river flowed past it and beneath the town wall, which curved away to both sides. The gate was built of huge planks of oak, four inches thick, with massive side pieces held in place by thick iron bolts hammered through and fastened on the other side. On each side of the gate there was a wooden tower also built of heavy oak, and surmounting each one, a cockpit with a pitched roof of elm shingles. A mailed watchguard in each holding a halberd with a fluttering red pennant. Atop each cockpit, another red pennant, the heraldic Tudor lion faintly visible in the hail-shower and the darkening light. Slowly the gates were pulled back to allow the riders in and for a moment they stood their horses under the portico. Mountjoy's sexual arousal had quietened; Penelope Rich was now a mere memory, not an inflammation of the nerves. He stayed there, under the gate, enjoyed the brief shelter and delay before entering the chamber down the muddy street in Christchurch.

O'Kelly was speaking of O'Neill's campaign in Munster. The chamber was lit by many candles, as daylight was now almost completely gone. They were seated at a long table, set with bowls of fruit and jugs of claret. Mountjoy tasted the wine again. It had begun to relax his throat. There were twenty or so men at the table, among them the Sheriff of Cork, the Lord President of Munster, Carew, merchants from the town – Coppinger, Morrow, Pate, Askew – and settlers from the countryside, among them, Chester, Walford, and the agents of Ralegh and Boyle.

All were drinking heavily, and had been even before Mountjoy had arrived. As soon as he'd entered, the silence of deference descended on the room. He'd yet to prove himself to these men, but they'd heard of him as a veteran of the Spanish Wars, how he'd fought with Sidney at Zutphen in the Low Countries, how his mistress, sister to the executed rebel, Robert Earl of Essex, had stood up to the Queen herself, boldly asserting her independence. Mountjoy knew they'd be thinking: anyone who can take a woman like that to bed, who would give her children, must be a force. He was said to be fearless of disgrace. Blount. Blunt. Others might practise studied melancholia, carefully rehearse nonchalance; his technique was ferocity. And silence. In Ireland silence always was a useful weapon. They didn't know how to wield it effectively. There was O'Kelly, for all his hauteur, talking too much when it came to it. The half-drunk assembly were still attentive, however.

'You see, gentlemen, it's not that there is amongst the general populace a great force for pushing toward a reckoning with England. I have spoken with certain men in this countryside who are members of the learned classes of the Gaelic poetic order (who also act as justiciars, of a sort) and they maintain that O'Neill's energy and victory derive from fear, not of his military valour but of his foxiness and the subtlety of his ever-increasing hate. Towards their masters, the chieftancies of the south, as well as the English. They maintain, also, that my Lord Mountjoy here is held in terror by O'Neill's men. They say Mountjoy is an engine of war. These men my lord and I met at a parley near the MacCarthy seat this yesterday night. We loosened their tongues with wine.'

Faces turned towards Mountjoy. A tanner called Gamble spoke: 'My lord, will you march against O'Neill and red-haired Tyrconnell? They are, even now, we understand, ravaging the lands of the O'Briens just north of the Shannon. They raid O'Brien's barns, and O'Neill himself extends his prerogative to sleep with anyone he desires, wife, or daughter, or boy. This insolence and rapacity, my lord, must be checked.'

'It will.'

'Will you march into north Munster?'

'Waiting is the chief art of warfare,' Mountjoy said. 'And silence.'

1956

MICHAEL CONDON

He closed the frosted-glass door of the bungalow. 'Padua'. In memory of Saint Anthony, a favourite saint of all the Condons. It was seven o'clock on a Sunday morning in May and the light was warm. Behind him the darkened house, curtains still drawn, the tap dripping into the glazed white sink, a clock ticking. His wife Teresa was still in bed, and his daughter Patricia asleep in the room next to theirs. He'd stopped to listen outside Patricia's door: her breathing was regular, but still not easy. He could hear a resonating rasp in her chest and knew that the infection hadn't shifted yet. The deep undertone to her breathing meant that the phlegm-encrusted walls of her little lungs were still vibrating with each effortful intake and exhalation. He was afraid.

Every morning now since the death he'd made the journey: seven long weeks, every day of them an agony of continuous recall. Teresa never asked him where he'd been each morning – she knew, but didn't want to bring it up. He'd be back in an hour, and she'd have the fire lit and they would be ready for Mass. The rashers and sausages lying in the aluminium pan to be cooked afterwards, eggs to one side on the cupboard, also in readiness.

Walking over the gravel to the blue van, he could hear the chimings of the Holy Trinity Church on Morrison's Island, faintly audible even at this distance from the city in the still calm air and warmth. When he got into the van it was stuffy with the heat and the smell of warm leather. He rolled down the window with difficulty, and had to ensure that it dropped gradually by holding its weight off the ratchets with the extended palm of his left hand. A breath of hawthorn blossom from the trees in the hedge drove into the van's interior. Even though the city was only two minutes away, this was still the country and when he turned left outside the gate he faced the van into a narrow lane, whitened along its verge by the milky hawthorn blossom. Its aroma was very strong – a tang in the air, an undercurrent of summer. He came to the lough and turned left up Hartland's Avenue. There was no traffic on the roads: he saw a man standing at the side of the water's edge, one foot on its low concrete kerb, looking at the swans paddling in the reeds around the island in the centre. Along Glasheen Road. Its villas had high stone walls. Through the occasional gate left ajar he'd see the shade created by a monkey puzzle tree; a white garden seat; a stained-glass front door, neatly grained with its brasses shining. On his forehead he felt the heat of the sun through the windscreen, and he was aware that the warmth was awakening the smell of the Brylcreem on his scalp and hair.

He parked outside the semicircular entrance walls and gates

of St Finbarr's cemetery. It was open, though at this hour no one else would be there, apart from the hunchbacked clerk with the stubby fingers in the apse-like office. To the right the republican plot, the great stone monument of the Sword of Light towering over the graves of fighters in the War of Independence.

Little Christopher's face came into his mind. The child lying white and still, except for his hands on the sheet turned down over the blankets. He kept on touching the cotton with the tips of his fingers, his eyes shut, as another wave of pain tore through him. Then the faint body gathered itself for another seismic cough. When it came the sheer volume of the sound made in that small breastbone, as the cough racked the child in its paroxysm, froze Michael as he sat there, the enamel kidney dish in his hand. He held it to Christopher's mouth as the seizure lessened, and he could hear the solid matter gurgling in the boy's throat. It filled the child's mouth, and then he spat out a large ball of bile, phlegm, and blood, flecked with particles of white that Michael knew were bits of lung. His son's face relaxed, and he didn't breathe for a while. When he did, the rasping, hollow grating told Michael that the pain was already beginning its build-up, which would soon result in another coughing fit and expectoration.

He prayed to Saint Anthony that he be taken and the boy spared. But it was impossible. Diphtheria. And everyone said no child got it any more. 'It's all right, boy,' he said. 'It's all right. You'll be fine. It won't be long until you're out playing on the high bees again behind the house. Chasing rabbits with Dandy. God is good.'

The child opened his eyes and looked at him. He was six, nearly seven. Michael loved having him in the van with him on Saturdays, taking him around to all his sisters: in every house a sweet, or a bite of cake. And then, even better, the journeys between the houses, where the boy would ask him questions about the produce. How did the farmers get the chickens to him? What happens to the pigs when they go to the factory? How were sausages made? And he'd answer every question in detail, because he believed it was good to encourage an enquiring mind. You'd never know. He might be a doctor or a priest. He'd reached the age of reason.

Christopher controlled his breathing for a moment so he could speak. He swallowed, then said: 'I know God is good, Daddy. And if I die, I'll pray for you and Mammy, and Patricia, and Aunty Kath and Aunty Ann, and everybody. And even Mr Holmes.' At that moment Michael Condon knew his heart was broken for ever, that he'd never again have a moment's peace.

He walked up the cinder pathway to the grave. No one knew, not even Teresa, what he'd been doing for seven weeks now. Three weeks of scrabbling and taking the clay away in his pocket, emptying it in the garden around the bungalow. Covering where he'd been working at the right-hand corner of the grave near the pathway with a flat stone, hidden by a layer of white marble chippings. For the last four weeks he'd been able to do what he had come again this morning to do. Kneeling down, he prayed again to Saint Anthony, and to the Mother of God, and asked forgiveness. He bent forward and scraped aside the chippings. He looked at his son's name on the headstone, the last in a list beginning with James Condon, 1848. He pushed the stone aside, and feeling the sun warming his blue serge jacket, he lowered his face to the kerb as he pushed his hand down the tunnel he had made to touch the timber of his son's coffin.

1924

KATHERINE CONDON

This is my last day at school. A Thursday in March, early March. The wind sharp and sleety, and the colour of the light going down Murphy's Lane is grey, that dark slate-blue grey that has the feel of snow to it. Last night I was up with Mrs Callaghan doing her ironing for her, as I do once a week, and having a talk with her. Not but that she does most of the talking. But on the way home with Thomas, her young fellow who's still at national school, he pointed out to me the stars and planets, giving some of them names. Jupiter, I remember, he called one; and Mars another; another, Orion. He knows a lot and he'll talk away like that without any embarrassment. The night was clear with frost and the moon was a sharp sickle in the sky. I like this cold; I like the freshness it brings and at this time of the year you can smell the growth in the plants as they begin to stir again after the winter. Tonight will be clear again, maybe.

This morning there was the usual fuss and nonsense in the house, with the men all noise and go. My brother Michael polishing his boots, one foot up on the chair just inside the kitchen door where I like to sit in quiet, talking away even though nobody listens to him. He has his own tin of black Dubbin that he keeps in the coal hole under the stairs, and every morning it's the same thing. The kitchen table has to be pushed back from the door of the coal hole, so he can reach his hand in and get out his brushes, tin and rags. Then there's his big backside blocking the way on everyone else, until he's satisfied that the job is done. And all the time going on about Mr Holmes this, and Mr Holmes that. How Tom Mull is in trouble, that Mr Holmes has latched on to the fact that the stock is being interfered with. How he said to Mr Holmes that not everyone is as honest as you might think, and how Morgan Holmes agreed with that. All the time the big arse of him stuck out as he polished up those boots of his, while he praises the leather in them and tells us for the umpteenth time how Drummy's is the only place for decent shoe leather. He's an old man's arse, and an old woman at one and the same time. Meanwhile, there's Ma over at the stove, wiping at the heavy iron pan with a bit of newspaper, then plopping in from the dripping mug a piece of fat which swims around on the hot black metal: the two rashers go in, one for Michael and the other for Da, who's sitting where he always sits, in the corner, quiet. He's nearly totally blind now. I got the fried bread, as ever, but it had the taste of the bacon on it. A lining for the stomach, Ma says.

I love the way Summerhill South turns around into the beginning of Douglas Street, and the horse trough there. The horses standing in their canvas coats, steamy breath coming out of their nostrils in thick jets when they raise their heads from the water. The South Presentation Convent is at the far end of Douglas Street, and at this hour many of the shops are already open. A man carrying a huge wooden tray of cakes from Thompson's delivery dray stops to let me past. He laughs at me and winks.

'Off to the holy nuns, are we? You should be away to Tin Pan Alley in New York where you'd turn everybody's head with that hair of yours.'

'Catch yourself on.'

A horse whinnies as I walk on down Douglas Street. At Bennett's, the hardware shop, I stop outside, and get the smell of carbolic soap and Jeyes Fluid, hemp mats, jute sacks of nails. Smells of iron and canvas. I look at myself in the window. Katherine Condon, fourteen, leaving school. I look at my dark, thick hair, naturally curled, the sallow skin. I wish I was fair. I'm happy with the eyebrows and lashes: the brows make a perfect clean curve over the eyelid, and my lashes jut right out in a heavy swoop. My eyes are deep brown, like a horse's eyes, I always think. Already I have a woman's body under my blue school shirt and old blazer, the uniform picked up in a jumble sale in Barrack Street for a tanner.

Mr Bennett, who is throwing sawdust on the wooden floor from a bucket, comes to the door. 'Don't be admiring yourself, Kath,' he says. 'The Condons were always as vain as they were good-looking. Do you know, your people came from the same part of north Cork as my mother's crowd, the Walshes, did?'

'I know, Mr Bennett.'

'You'll be late for school, you know, if you don't hurry along.'

'It's my last day.'

'Well, thanks be to God. And I remember you a little thing in your mother's arms at Mass in the convent. And what are you doing?'

'I've a job in the new laundry on the South Main Street.'

'The Jewman's?'

'Yes.'

'Well, good luck to you.'

He sets the bucket down, and, after wiping his hand on his old brown overall, he extends it to me, and I take it. He shakes it warmly and clasps it with his other hand, which is soft and dry.

I go through the stone gateway to the convent. The children have already gone in; it is later than I'd thought. The classroom is warm after the cold.

English. I've read my story. About nothing. About coming in from Bishopstown carrying a Rexine bag of apples from the orchard, and, sitting on top of them, a barmbrack cake cooked on the griddle over the open fire by my grandmother. My grandmother, smoking Clarke's Perfect Plug, blowing out of her toothless gums the bright blue smoke. That was it, the story.

'Katherine,' says Sister Therese (I love her because she's gentle and softly spoken and has fair skin), 'that is a lovely story. You've very good at English.'

'But, Sister,' I say, 'it's not a story. I'm no good at making things up.'

'A good story should never be like something made up,' said Sister Therese. 'It should be as if it were happening to us as we hear it. Girls,' she said, smiling at the class, 'didn't you all see Katherine walking along with the bag of apples, standing outside the door of her house, waiting for a moment before she went in? Why did you wait outside before going in with the cake and the apples?'

'I don't know, Sister.'

'It's because you wanted to think about what you were doing, to just wait for a while and let your feelings calm down. But your story half tells us why you did what you did; and at the same time keeps us guessing. And that's a good story.'

'But it's not a story, Sister; it's only what I did.'

'Exactly,' says Sister Therese, and she opens her pale red lips and smiles.

'Katherine,' she says, 'you are a storyteller. Promise me you'll always read books. Girls, you all know that Katherine is leaving today to go to work. It is a great pity. She's good at English, and she sews beautifully. If you ever feel you might have a vocation, Katherine, please come and see me, or any of the Sisters in the convent. We'll pray for you, for God to watch over you and guide you.'

She comes down to me where I sit at my desk, my hands joined beneath it sweating with embarrassment. She puts her small hand on my head and gives my hair a gentle stroke. Everybody loves Sister Therese. We know she is good: she never shouts at us, or tries to catch us out in our lies. We run to open the door for her when she leaves the room, and when we see her coming along the corridor we rush to open it for her. All the girls love the English classes and the sewing classes. She looks down at me and I see there is water in her eyes. Immediately I am crying and sobbing so much I cannot stop. I wish I could love everyone the way I love Sister Therese.

'We'll say a decade of the rosary for Katherine,' she says, turning away, and even in my tears I can smell her cleanly smell, of violets and daffodils, and of grass in the summer in the long fields outside Bishopstown.

1586

LODOWICK RICHE

TO MY DEARLY LOVED AND HONOURED FRIEND, THE MOST
DIGNIFIED GENTLEMAN, MASTER SPENSER, NEWLY INSTALLED
CLERK TO THE ROYAL COUNCIL OF MUNSTER UNDER THE GRACIOUS
AUTHORITY OF HER MAJESTY, AND FOR HIS CONVEYANCE TO SIR
JOHN NORRYS, PRESIDENT OF THE SAME BODY, TO BE CONSIDERED
AT THE NEXT SESSIONS IN CORK.

Most esteemed and honoured gentleman:

I am compelled to write to you, in the clear and decided
knowledge that you will remit these my sorry reports to Sir
John, President of that body charged with the settling of this

most troubled territory, so that you in your wisdom and goodness and President Norrys in his calm adjudications may be fully apprized how desperate my life has been these last weeks. I speak of the tribe of the Condons, who, inflamed with the passions of rebellion and usurpation, have left discarded any small trace of pity or remorse that may once have had a seat in their affections, although the witness of my own eyes, and the sorrowful recollections of my heart, do not allow me to think that these ever had any sway in their tempestuous feelings. They are governed only by their will, which they ever confine to the constraints of hate and the inclinations of slaughter.

Three nights past, my wife and I and our three children being abed, these miscreants stole from their boggy places and fens, and, enshrouded in darkness, came to our doors, a small multitude of them, shrieking at us, in the vilest English, their speech besmirched with their broguish deformities. They clamoured at us poor creatures, now awakened from our slumber and gathered quaking before the dying embers of the fire in the hearth in the humble room that served us as our eating hall and chamber of assembly, where we would meet and plan together the order of our lives under the benign protection of Her Sacred Majesty. Now at our doors and windows were the shoutings of this rabblement, whose continuous burden was 'Cundoon', 'Cundoon', the Erse for the name which will ever now be associated with brutish terror and nightmarish outlawry. A pike came through the stout timbers of the main door and the visage of a dark-skinned wretch could be seen, his blackened teeth most fitting in his blackamoor face. My wife was now in a piteous state, and all the restraints of nature had deserted her and my poor children. Her fear was intermixed with disgrace that I should be a witness to the involuntary spasms of their bodies in the seizure of horror. I had prepared and hung upon the wall a firing piece charged with ball and powder and with all speed I took it and fired the instrument at the blackamoor's face. The discharge made a terrible noise and before the smoke beclouded all the chamber I saw the face recoiling, made a shambles of gore. The tumult of this shot and the confusion made widespread by the smoke brought about a respite of silence as the Condon wretches cowered in fear of further discharges. I told my wife to gather our little compact of humanity with her up the stairs and to lock herself in the linen room. Some few minutes passed by in this burdensome quiet, but then, with a fierce and ursine roar, these Condons redoubled their shoutings and animadversions, using the foulest epithets in sullying the goodness and purity of Her Majesty, our Gracious Queen. I cannot record what they said, for most of what they screamed was in Irish, but they made vile accusations pertaining to her sacred person, laughing and scorning her the while. Whatever your honours may imagine to be the most bestial acts a woman may commit, such were the substance of the calls and halloos they urged at me through the many apertures they had now broken through in our doors and windows. The main postern gave way to their puissant force and momently our chamber was filled with these brutes and the milk-like stink of their unwashed bodies. One of their horde, who, though wearing about his person a voluminous cloak fastened at the neck with a brooch of some golden stuff, was naked else, pushed forward and by his pride and arrogance proclaimed himself their leader, if such an unruly band could ever allow anyone any command or supremacy. Boldly he stood before me, careless that his manhood, in the excitement of rage and conquest, was stirring. I covered my eyes with my hands so as not to have to gaze on such a display. He spoke to me in a halting English to say that these were his lands, from the time of Noah, or some such, and that he would not kill us all on this occasion, only show my wife the force of Irish manhood, and take my eldest daughter to be his concubine in his wild fastnesses. A few ragged men started up the stairs and found where my treasured ones were by their wailings and prayers. I need not further describe how this scene continued, to the endless distress and sorrow of my mind. It is a harsh Commandment of our Saviour that we love our enemies and, good Sirs, it is one I cannot obey again. I pray I may be released from this sin, but I also pray for vengeance on those vicious brutes who watched while this naked rebel urged himself upon my trembling and shaking wife. I had to witness the most shameful sight that must befall a husband to see, and this Condon, Terence his name, proffered to me, in the midst of his pleasuring, a dirk, saying that I could bring a surcease to my fortune by my own hand, should I find the sight too disagreeable. If I did not, he warned, then he could only conclude that the sight was not totally displeasant to me, saying further that he was well aware of our English furtiveness and clandestine pleasures. After slaking his vicious desire, he then took my eldest child, Rosalind, along with him out the door, impervious to her beseechings, and laughing at me, said, that in a season she would not wish ever to cross my threshold again, so much would she become enamoured of his Irish freedom. He told me to quit my lands or all my family would be put to the sword, but not before they had each of them been violated by him and his lieutenants in conquest. Next morning we quit our house and took ourselves to the road with a few chattels, leaving the plains beneath the Galtee Mountains I had grown to be fond of, in the Glen of Aherlow, to the greater though not impregnable safety of the town of Fermoy, where I have lodgings through the kindness of a generous and Christian gentleman of the town, whose heart was moved by the piteousness of our condition. I know not where my Rosalind is, or if she still lives in this caitiff's captivity. I beseech you, Master Spenser, to recollect the firmness of the most high Lord Grey of Wilton, whose iron decision is greatly lamented, and who closely understood these bitter hearts, having had cause to study their devices and strategies. Visit, I pray you, Sir John, the most ardent cruelties on the rebels in the Galtees and in Aherlow. Nothing will stop them save the steady application of the most forceful suppression made fast by remorseless anger and revenge. Where charity resides in all of this is not for us to ponder, save that the making tender these hard hearts by rude and unconfined punishment must be the prelude to the working of the grace of our most Blessed Saviour. I pray you, gentlemen, kill these rebels. I am your obedient servant in tribulation, and yet expectant of hope:

LODOWICK RICHE,
FREEHOLDER AT KILBEHENY IN THE PROVINCE OF MUNSTER,
NOW RESIDENT AT FERMOY,
IN THE YEAR OF OUR LORD, 1586, THE SIXTH DAY OF MARCH

1920

TOM MULL

Tom Mull lived up on Blarney Street, a part of the city
virtually unknown to Michael Condon, who came from the
Southside, beyond the South Gate Bridge. The Northside lay
beyond the corresponding North Gate Bridge, flanked by
quays on either side. It was twelve o'clock on a Sunday, and
Shandon church rang out the midday tolling, a mixture of
trebles and deeper notes drifting over the quiet on sunny and
near empty streets. A few late Mass-goers hurried along the
quay to St Mary's, the Dominican priory. The 'drunkard's
Mass' was what Michael's mother called high Mass, implying
that anyone who had to resort to this 'long-drawn-out affair'

did so because last night's hectic drinking compelled them to the lengthy sermon, the sung Latin liturgy, the dreary ceremonial. Michael had, as ever, been at eight o'clock Mass at the convent with his mother, something he had done since childhood. She had taught him how to pray, so that now it was something he did a great deal of the time, without thinking of it. His mind always turned to God and to His Blessed Mother, and not necessarily because he wanted something, it was just an impulse of his thought and feeling, exactly as he knew it to be for his mother.

The day was warm and bright, but would occasionally darken as slow-moving August clouds blotted out the sun for ten minutes or more. Then the city streets grew sombre; a grey cat prowling along the wall tipped with broken glass set in concrete would fill him with unease and sadness. Why, he did not know. He noticed he was growing more susceptible to these mood changes lately: maybe it was part of growing up. He didn't feel grown up; nor did he feel like a child, either. He had long left childhood behind in any case: his father's increasing blindness made him, as the eldest, the head of the house. He'd begun to take on that role some years ago, anyway, even while his father's sight was still reasonably good, because everyone knew that a drinking man could scarcely look after himself, let alone a family. He knew his da's battering rages, his weeping, his uselessness had long ago lost him any respect he'd held in his mother's eyes. Now Ma just barely put up with the 'old fellow' (as she called him). He remembered yesterday's awful lunch. Saturday. He was home from Holmes's at one thirty, the only day in the week apart from Sunday that he had dinner at home. They were all there: him, the sisters Ann, Sarah, Kath, and his brothers Con and Tom, as well as the da. They had pulled out the small table and the older ones were seated at it, but the younger children were sitting or standing as best they could in the kitchen and in the pink painted hallway and at the bottom of the stairs. The potatoes were in the middle of the table, with a jar of dripping kept from last Sunday's roast meat, and on the plates were portions of pig meat – morsels for the little ones, larger pieces for the older, the biggest of all for him.

His father, Jim, sat in the darkest corner of the kitchen, squeezed between the stove and the coal hole, his hands lying quietly on the table, waiting for the sounds of eating to begin so he would know when the food was up. Kath had already peeled his potatoes for him and swabbed a dollop of dripping over them before salting them. The meat was boiled backbones and tail ends of cured pig; after cooking, the flesh, sparse on the complicated bones, was red and flaky and had to be sucked off. His wife half threw a tiny portion of the fattest part of the tail end, all white coagulation, onto her husband's plate, and they began to eat.

At first there was just the clanking sound of knives and forks, the sucking of warm meat off the bones, and the crunching of the soft cartilage itself. Then, taking the fatty bone from his lips covered in dripping and pig fat and laying it on the side of his plate, having felt for its round shape on the table, Jim spoke. 'Jesus, this is all fat, and rotten fat, too, with no taste to it, Mary. Is this the kind of meat to put before me?'

'Eat what the good Lord provided for you and don't complain,' his wife replied.

'There's no call for you to speak to me like that; and I'm entitled to the best that's in this house. I bet you that cute bastard Mikey has the best of the bacon, the scut.'

'Keep a civil tongue in your head, you,' said Mary.

The meal continued in silence; the eating, sucking and clanking sounds beginning again. But after a period of dread and unease and uncertainty, the father began once more.

'This is the thanks I get from you, you ungrateful bitch, when I sacrificed my life for you and your filthy offspring. Every year another brat. You're a rabbit, that's what you are, a bloody rabbit.'

'This is a terrible way to talk in front of the children.'

Michael's rage was growing all the time. He wanted to catch

that bony piece of flesh on his father's plate and shove it down his gullet. Blast him and his damned useless eyes.

'Look here, you,' he said to his father. 'There's no fat on that meat before you. Eat it up and be quiet and be satisfied.' He knew he had the best of the pig meat, but didn't he deserve it? Not like that blind, played-out old man, who was only good for drinking whatever money he could lay his hands on.

As he began the ascent up Shandon Street the sun came out again, and he saw fluttering on a newspaper display board outside a closed-up shop, a handwritten notice about the arrest of the Lord Mayor of Cork: 'Terence MacSwiney Taken in Raid on City Hall'. He turned left up Blarney Street, the longest street in Ireland, someone once had told him, and walked along the pavement with its smooth sandstone kerbs. The Mulls lived in a house set back from the street. He went through a passageway smelling of cabbage and drinkers' piss, with doors off to other houses and flats. A sour smell.

He walked into a courtyard with small cottage-type houses ranged round on three sides. The remaining side of the yard was a waist-high wall, looking down into a stone quarry, and beyond it the city, the Mardyke, Sunday's Well, and the university. A high pavement fronted all of the houses, and beneath this and before the dwellings was a cobbled yard. In a corner were some stables and the horses raised their heads to look at him when he came into the quiet enclosure. The stables and a few of the houses had thatched roofs of straw, held in place by large stones hanging from hempen ropes. Houses and stables had half-doors, and the upper parts of most of these were open to the fine day. There were the smells of cooking: bacon, roast meat, the musky odour of potatoes boiling. An old man in shirt sleeves sat outside one door, smoking a clay pipe; outside another a heavy woman in a blue overall wound wool into a ball from a skein off the hands of a young boy, who held them up to her, moving them as the wool slipped off each in turn. Tom looked out over his half-door, and called Michael's name, inviting him in.

The interior of the thatched cottage was warm. It was now bright sunlight outside and Michael found it difficult at first to make out who was in the room. Tom's mother was standing at the big open hearth, the only means of cooking in the house. Her feet were bare, and with a shock Michael saw that her legs were filthy up to her overall. A black shawl with a large hood hung on a peg by the door. Even here, inside, her head was covered with a bright red scarf. Tom's father Patrick sat in the nook in the hearth and watched his wife as she lifted the black pot to smell the pot roast.

'It's nearly done,' she said, 'and the spuds are coming along well, too, and the leeks and onions are starting to melt down, the way you like them, Tom.'

Tom had seated himself at the kitchen table, his long legs were stretched out, and his arm lay along the oilcloth, touching the knives and forks at the places set for dinner. His bald head gleamed above his tonsure of hair.

'Have you the peas on too?' asked Patrick.

'It'll all be ready quite soon,' she said. And then she started talking to her husband in Irish.

Outside of school Michael had never heard anybody speak this language. 'I didn't know, Tom, that you were Irish speakers.'

'We're not that,' said Tom. 'It's just that Ma and Da come from out Carrignavar and Whitechurch way, where there was still a bit of Irish when they were growing up. And they still use it, don't you, Ma? Although I don't have any of it myself.'

'No use to anyone anyway,' growled Patrick, pulling his cap down over his eyes. 'A sickening language that ever only brought us misery. Thanks be to God that Tom knows not one syllable of it. Poverty and hardship is all it ever bloody well brought to any of us. It's all very well for the likes of MacSwiney and his friends to be oohing and aahing about it, but I remember well my father telling me about old Long out in Carrignavar begging the leavings of the table for his five children, and him living in a cave, yes, a cave, with his poor

slattern of a wife. The children, they used to say, died on him
one by one. And the poor man; when he'd get a drink into him
he'd go on and on to my father about the manuscripts of this
and that, and how he could trace the Mull family back to some
old Dane that landed in Cork, and how we were a very old and
fine family.'

'Isn't that why I married you,' said Mrs Mull, as she spun
round quickly, as brisk as a girl, from the fire.

She was now making the gravy, having lifted out the roast
beef trussed in butcher's string and placed it and the vegetables
on a plate beside the glowing turf. She sifted some flour into
the juices in the pot, then stirred, then threw in some water
off the simmering peas, and poured the thick brown liquid into
a long blue gravy boat. The roast was sliced into cuts an inch
thick and all four of them were given a plate with meat, gravy,
potatoes, peas, and leek and onion mix.

Michael had never had gravy before in his life and he
wondered at the taste. In fact, he had never eaten food like this
before. Overcoming his shyness, he said: 'They wouldn't get
this in the Victoria Hotel.'

All three of the Mulls laughed. A wild laughter that set the
horses whinnying in the stables outside, and drew from the old
man sitting along the pavement, and smoking, the following:
'Would you lot of Mulls eat in peace and leave us in peace.
And if there's any left, those smells have been making my
mouth water and I'd only be too happy to oblige.'

This, thought Michael, is what it might be like to be happy.
Patrick Mull had one of the meanest livelihoods in the city: he
gathered up kitchen waste and refuse in his donkey and cart all
over the town – potato skins, carrot tops, turnip heads, slop,
onion peelings – and took them out to his sheds along the far
end of Blarney Street, where he kept a few pigs. He'd sell them
to Murphy's or Lunham's bacon factories once in a while; and
that was how he survived. No one knew how he kept his
family fed on that paltry income, and his feats of survival were
a constant topic of conversation in the houses he visited. He

never rode on the cart to spare his donkey, and he'd talk to her all the time. People said he and all the Mulls were a bit soft in the head. If they were, Michael thought, they knew how to look after themselves and other people.

1836

MICHAEL LONG

I am sorely troubled that the meagre inheritance I can leave my sons is the poor remnant of my learning and ability. I care little for what the world can do to me now, because so harsh and unremitting have been its sufferings that I am proof against its rancours. My emotions range very narrowly and mostly in the confines of hate. I still hate now, and me an old man, with a passion and ferocity that sometimes appals even myself. I seem to rage against everything but those dearest to me in love, and the memory of my dead wife. I am harrowed by the thought of what fortune holds for my two boys, whose intellects and hands I have striven so much to discipline. But what use will there ever be again for the learning imparted to me in Limerick and the schools of Cork and which I, through want of teachers adequate to the task, have had to undertake in the case of my own two boys? I am back again where I started twenty years ago, and that renovation then nearly broke my strength. I was nearing fifty years of age at that time, and instead of beginning to experience the calmness of content and achievement, I had to begin to forage all over again for my living. I am subsisting now, as I was then, in a miserable tent, made of sackcloth, abutting into a cave outside Carrignavar. It is scarcely credible that someone such as I, well known and respected for the care and the scruple of my learning, should now find myself without a single name of substance to provide me with what little I need to live. My two boys are now men in their maturity, and they must be content to get what they can in the way of day-labouring wages. When I look at those hands calloused and blistered from the hayfork and spade, and when I think that those fingers are still capable of transcribing the tales and sagas of Ulster and Munster and the poetry of Dallán Forgaill in a script that retains all the elegance and clarity it had when men of learning wrote it in the time of Saint Patrick, then my heart fills with black rage and hatred. I look at my two men-children, early in the morning, as they sleep, exhausted from their exertion of the previous day, their mouths wide open, as the breath from their bodies smokes in the freezing air of the cave. The condensation on the walls, from the heat of our bodies, runs down in dark, stained rivulets. Twenty years ago they were huddled together, with their sisters and brother, clung to each other in damp warmth against the ferocious cold. I wrote out my misery then; I write it out now. For no one to read. In the name of Jesus and His Blessed Mother, I call upon you, Almighty God the Father, to revenge my suffering people. May their enemies be laid in the dust, their mouths agape at the righteous terror of the Lord, who knows, in His wisdom, that there are times when nothing will do but to intermit His Divine Mercy and visit directly in their lives the consequences of their actions upon the wicked.

MICHAEL LONG,
CARRIGNAVAR,
SCRIBE AND SCHOOLMASTER,
THIS DAY OF OUR LORD, FIRST DECEMBER 1836

1930

KATHERINE CONDON

Mr Jacob Sless was sitting at his desk when I went in out of the steam of the washroom. I brushed the hair off my forehead that was falling down in front of my eyes with the damp and the sweat. I was slightly out of breath, as I'd just been lifting sheets out of the big boiling vats and my hands were red from their scalding heat. We had large wooden paddles to pull them out with, but they're no good and more trouble than they're worth: you have to climb up on a small stepladder and get your hands under their heavy weight before you can get them out. You could spend ten minutes foostering with the lifting paddles and get nowhere at all. And I hate delay and waste of time, which is why Mr Sless respects me, and why I'm charge hand in the laundry at only twenty years of age. It's never happened before that someone so young has been given the job of leading a team of four others, and all of them older than me. Mrs Hennessy, from the Marsh, is as old as my mother. I've been a charge hand for over a year now.

'Katherine,' says Mr Sless, 'do please sit down.'

He still talks in a funny accent, even though, as he's told me many times, he's been in Cork since he was a child. He refers to himself as the Cork Jew, which he seems to find humorous. And when he says that, he'll go off chuckling to himself, and repeating it under his breath.

'This is Friday, payday, as you know, and I want to just show you how pleased I am with how hard you've been working by giving you a little something for yourself, and something, too, for your mother. Here: this is for Mrs Condon, who is a very nice and kind lady.'

He has before him on the desk a small blue box, which he opens, and pushing aside the tendrils of straw, he lifts out a little figurine: a small shepherdess with a hook, in indigo glass, and a lamb beside her on the small circular base. At her feet there are unevennesses, coloured grey, that suggest stones or rocky ground.

'This is from my father's town in Hungary,' he says, 'a place called Pécs, where they make the most beautiful glass. Indeed, my father was the chemist and the colour-mixer in the very factory which made this before he and my mother had to leave. Such a long time ago now. The owner helped my parents and got them out of the country. Such bad times. But let us not talk of that. What do you think of the present? Do you think your mother will like it?'

'I know she'll be mad about it, Mr Sless. She loves ornaments and she has a special cabinet for them in the front room. This one will be lovely there.'

My mother's special treat, on Saturdays, when all the men were out of the house, and Da getting drunk again, is to take out all her ornaments, gathered over the years from second-hand shops, fairgrounds, off barrows on the Coal Quay, and wash them one by one in water lathered with carbolic soap, and dry them on a tea towel, then shine them with a soft woollen sock.

'I'm very pleased that you think she'll like this. I asked my brother to pick it out specially for her.'

Mr Sless's brother has a hardware and household goods shop forty yards down the South Main Street from where the laundry is, at the corner with Washington Street. Half the houses of the poorer people in Cork are furnished by Sless, because he gives credit at a reasonable rate. If you need something and go into his shop, he will not leave you go without it. Some deal or other will be struck, some payment system fixed. So the word is, you have to be sure you want what you look at in Sless's.

'And now for you, dear Katherine.' He calls me 'dear' which embarrasses me a little, but only a little, because I know he means no harm: it is just his way. Maybe that's how they speak in Hungary. 'I want you to know,' he says, 'how much I value what you have been doing here. You are a good girl, and well-reared by that fine lady, your mother. You respect your elders, and you are a good Christian.'

I think of the catcalls I'll sometimes hear being shouted after him in the street, especially on Fridays at six o'clock, as he'd be walking along to his brother's shop, the louts hanging around Beamish's brewery singing out: 'Jew-boy, Jew-boy.'

'This is for you.' He hands me a long yellow envelope made of thick heavy paper. I open it and draw out two notes: ten pounds, four weeks' wages. 'A bonus,' he says. 'And tomorrow we celebrate the Feast of the Passover; do you know what happened then, and why we remember it every year?'

'Has it something to do with the Feast of the Lamb? Is it connected to Easter in the Catholic Church?'

I do not know what their lives are like. The synagogue on South Terrace is grey and foreign-looking. The Star of David in iron over the large maroon-painted door. The windows black and sad. I know Mr Sless and his brother Cecil live with their families in two big houses opposite each other on the Front Douglas Road, and old Mrs Sless, who is still alive, is living with Jacob, the eldest, who runs the laundry, and who is being kind to me now.

'The Passover is special for us Jews,' he says. 'It recalls the time when we were delivered safely out of our captivity in Egypt, when the Angel of Death passed over the houses of the Jews but killed all the first-born of the Egyptians. He passed over because he saw the sign: the blood of a lamb sprinkled, with hyssop, on the lintels and doorposts of the houses of the Jews. Tomorrow Cecil and I will eat a roast lamb with unleavened bread, as we are told to do in the Scriptures. I'd like your mother and you to visit us in Douglas sometime. Not tomorrow. That's for family, but some other time.'

I do not know what to say. I've never had in my hands such an amount of money before. I know Ma will have many uses for all of it, but with the figurine from Mr Sless there is a good chance she'll let me keep some of it, at least. I could not imagine what it would be like to be a visitor at the Sless house in Douglas. I could envisage my mother's face, tight with tension, calling Mr Sless 'your honour' with every second breath.

'That would be very nice,' I say. It is all I can think of saying.

I go back out into the steam and noise of the laundry. The girls in the ironing room at the top are waving their arms, posturing in mocking, suggestive attitudes, sticking their tongues out and calling at me. I cannot hear what they say with the roar of the huge gas jets under the aluminium vats and, in any case, they are behind a glass partition, so they look like actors in a dumb show. I join my own team, who are flapping two long sheets free of excess moisture before putting them into the drying room.

'Did old Sless give you the eye? I wonder what it would be

like with a circumcised fellow?' says Mrs Hennessy. 'I suppose
they're cleaner, more hygenic. But it must be a funny sight.'

'Take your mind off that kind of thing. It's easy known you
come from the Marsh with talk like that,' says Sally, from up
Barrack Street.

'Listen to her,' says Mrs Hennessy. 'That crowd in Barrack
Street wouldn't give you the steam off their piss.'

Sally, laughing, takes hold of a towel in the boiling vat and
swings its heavy steaming length, catching Mrs Hennessy a wet
slap to the thighs.

1902

MARY O'DWYER

The big windows had been thrown open on their cords to cool the classroom. The noise and bustle of the South Mall drifted up: footsteps; the clanging of a tram as it shunted on its lines; the inscrutable bawl of the newspaper boys; shouted greetings from one side of the street to the other; bits of conversations. Through the windows also drifted the smell of roasted coffee beans, pervasive always on the South Mall in the mornings, coming from Thompson's Restaurants and Tea Rooms, the Imperial Hotel, and the Cork and County Club.

Mary O'Dwyer looked out the window and yawned. The day was warm, but being still springtime, the air had a slight undercurrent of ice in it. She could feel the coolness in her lungs. Miss O'Sullivan was talking to them about interview etiquette for girls, how to make that initial and all-important first impression, how to enter a room, how to walk to the chair, how you should wait by the chair until invited to sit, how the purse should be placed on the floor beside the chair, how it should not, emphatically *not*, be put on the interview table.

Mary wondered about Miss O'Sullivan's underwear: where did she get it? was it expensive silk stuff from Grant's (she thought it might be) or was it just the plain old cotton stuff from Kinahan's on Oliver Plunkett Street that had those huge great pink corsets in the window and stays like horses' saddles? She imagined what she fancied Miss O'Sullivan would be wearing against her skin which always smelt of sweet – no, not sweet, fragrant perfumes. She liked her black clothes, quite severe, and thought how, underneath, the thin cords of the stays would be tied at the small of her back, and how, holding up the sheer stockings, the fasteners would press against her long, warm thighs. Her head was turned slightly to one side, so that the sun was shining directly onto her clear face. She had her eyes shut, and continued to swing her right leg slowly as she spoke.

'Girls,' she said, in her refined but definite voice, 'I want you always to remember that you go out of here as ambassadors (ambassadresses, I should say really) of this school. Your parents have made sacrifices that you could come here; we are not cheap. And you should repay them, and Taylor's Secretarial Academy, with your good manners and disciplined attention to whatever tasks are assigned to you. And,' she said, merrily, 'don't let the men get you in clinches in the broom cupboard, or don't let them insist on picking up a pencil you may have dropped while taking dictation. They're demons, girls, demons.'

The girls in the final year of training at Taylor's loved it when Miss O'Sullivan strayed off like this from the formal

instructional mode she did so well into this mockery of it.
They all laughed.

'Oh Miss. Are they? Tell us. How do you know?' said
Mary's deskmate, Claire Murphy, a blonde with peachy skin,
ash-grey hair, and green eyes, which now flashed at Mary in
cool mischief.

'You'll know soon enough, Miss Murphy, if you don't
know already. But, make no mistake about it, men are pred-
ators. They hunt. Anywhere, any time. And it's as well you
know that. I don't go along with what a lot of you will have
been taught by the good and holy nuns – that it's the girl's
responsibility to hold a man in check, because once they start
they can't stop. Goodness help them, the poor creatures.'

By now every face in the class of sixteen–seventeen-year-olds
was rapt with attention. A communal giggle flew round the
room.

'It's up to them to hold back, too. And women are just as
frail, or, if you like, just as passionate as men. We have feelings,
too, girls. No. But you've got to watch them, because (and
don't tell anyone I said this) there's a certain part of them that
has no memory and no conscience whatsoever.'

The class exploded into mirth. Mary looked sideways
at Claire and they both collapsed onto their arms on the
desk tops, bleating with laughter. Miss O'Sullivan tried, half-
heartedly, to calm them down, but she, too, was heaving
uncontrollably. Sitting up, still laughing, Mary looked out on
to the street. People were stopping in the bright sunshine and
looking up at the open windows of Taylor's, smiling at the riot
of gleeful sound.

After a few minutes and a number of ripples and gusts of
hilarity recurring involuntarily, Miss O'Sullivan began to speak
again, even though she, too, continued to be helplessly invaded
by the aftermath of the paroxysm. 'Oh dear,' she giggled. 'I've
got all hot.' This nearly started them off again, but she smacked
the edge of her desk with her bracelet, sharply. 'Seriously girls,
the interviews are coming up and the most respectable and

most long-established firms' – again she suppressed a raft of giggles in her chest and felt the hot tears of laughter in her eyes – 'and best businesses all take most of their secretarial staff from Taylor's Academy. And I've got here a list of interviewees for various firms: Mary O'Dwyer: Holmes's Hardware and Export Stores; Claire Murphy: Beamish's brewery; Andrea O'Mahony: MacCarthy/Morrogh – brokers; Nancy Fleming: Cork Steam Packet; Philomena O'Regan: Tedcastle's Coal. You must understand that we only send one candidate for each interview. Taylor's knows its clients' needs and chooses a girl who will fit to the working practices of the people who run the firm. They rely on us to make careful judgements and to spare them the nuisance of interviewing when they know we are in a better position to meet their requirements because we know our girls – yes, you are better than they could ever hope to get on the basis of an interview. So Taylor's reposes its trust in you and hopes that you will not besmirch' – at this Miss O'Sullivan smirked – 'the good name of your Alma Mater. You are, girls, the cream of professional women in Cork, destined, if you play your cards close to your chests' – giggles again – 'for lawn tennis parties, the golf links, the Royal Yacht Club, and being tormented by eager young men who can't keep their hands off you.'

Once more they all laughed. Miss O'Sullivan thought of the black hair of George Twomey, her young man, importuning her to marry him, as he nuzzled his face between her breasts last Sunday on a riverbank at Iniscarra. The River Lee turning away from where they sat, a green expanse, brilliant in the sun. Behind them, a small Protestant church with its vaulted crypt, the thin, mullioned windows keeping the air fresh as it blew around the quiet lead coffins. The sight of the vault had persuaded her to give into his urgings that she bare her breasts for him. But watching him, in his despairing passion, she realised she had bared them for herself as much as for him. Why, she did not know. If men were strange, women were stranger.

Mary O'Dwyer pondered the name 'Holmes'. She thought of a man's head just visible above a hawthorn hedge and on top of it, jauntily, a white sailor's cap.

1886

RANDALL HERBERT

Randall Herbert walked back up the narrow gravel pathway connecting his house with the church. His father, Crawford, had the little oratory built when Randall was a boy, and he loved the round tower at its far end, a perfect miniature in red stone of the tower on Devenish Island in County Fermanagh. Every morning when he walked down to the church to say his prayers he would recall that boat trip out to Devenish when he was thirteen, his father telling him how these towers were famous all over Europe, that they were unique to Ireland. That was why he'd insisted, despite the bafflement of the architects in Cork at his extravagance, on including one in his oratory. He wanted to build a small version of a medieval Irish monastery, with bare, flagged floors, pews of oak finely planed, and stained glass with deep hues of blue and green. He had done so, and Randall knew how proud his father was that he had created, in his own mind, something of lasting architectural value in Cappoquin.

'In time,' his father had said to Randall as they rode out in the small skiff to Devenish, the island bare and empty apart from the sheep which cropped its vivid green grass to a close and even lawn, 'in time people will appreciate again the old and austere styles of building. And they will see that a church or a house needs to be built with simplicity and with a view to its uses. Prayer is a cleansing of the mind, and the places we build for prayer should reflect this purifying function. People will come to see that our little oratory, in County Waterford, was a significant moment in arriving at a new honesty in building.'

Randall paused and looked at the Chinese lantern bush, the dark-red pendulous flowers just beginning to form at the end of the long drooping stems. His father had laid the pathway and planted the shrubs alongside. The mahonias, with their yellow flowers emitting a harsh astringent perfume, were nearly over. The air was still. He remembered his father's face on that boat trip, his profile turned aside, facing into the wind that agitated the lake. He recalled how sure and certain his father was: how he just knew he was right about architecture, planting, the management of the house. Crawford Herbert had, once, to the horror and amazement of his wife, decided that the carpets be removed from the floors and the timbers be stripped of all wax and paint by spreading on them a thick layer of carbolic soda mixed with flour and water. The cleaned wood was then washed and scrubbed, allowed to dry, and the boards fed with linseed oil and beeswax. 'We now,' he said to his wife after they moved back into the drawing room out of the servants' quarters in the basement, 'have the best yew floors in the south of Ireland.'

Randall walked into the hallway of the house, its yellow floor gleaming softly in the morning light. The door to the library was open, and there standing, looking at the book shelves, his back towards him, was Scully, the estate manager. He'd forgotten that Scully had sent a message last night that he needed to see him this morning. The wine again. Randall looked with unease at the heavy blue broadcloth of Scully's coat. He turned towards him as he heard Randall enter, and as he passed Scully to stand by the window he got the milky smell of his body heat. Scully's coat was open and his waistcoat unbuttoned. He was still warm from the exertion of riding, but he was nervous as well.

Randall looked out the window, down towards the oratory and, beyond it, the lake amidst the trees, where the pike swam in the cold water. Would it not be better, he thought, to be anything other than what we are; to be any other form of life? A pike experiencing the entire presence of the water, luxuriant in its knowing strength; its huge jaws. He turned to Scully. 'Well, Pat, what's the news? Did you meet them?'

'Yes, I met MacCarthy and Collins, those two trouble-making bastards. Mr Scully this, Mr Scully that. Oh, yes, we understand his honour's difficulties, but we have our problems too. And Father O'Flaherty says. And so on. You can imagine the whine of them and the cringing, whingeing obsequiousness of them. Oh, they wouldn't dream of causing trouble, only that, you know, Mr Davitt said this, and Parnell said that. I'm heartily sick of the lot of them. Land League is right. They're in league with Old Nick himself it seems to me. Why the hell they don't lock Parnell up for good and throw away the key, I don't know.'

'But Pat,' said Herbert, 'what's the outcome? Did you settle?'

'I made an offer.'

'And?'

'I offered a twenty-five per cent reduction in the rents.'

'Twenty-five per cent? That's too much. I don't know that I

can cope with that.'

Randall thought of the amount against him in the Munster and Leinster Bank in Youghal, and of the mortgages in Cork and Dublin. Five hundred thousand, in all, his attorney O'Kane had said, in his musty office on the South Mall in Cork. He pushed away his memory of O'Kane's sleek head and little moustache. The bottle of sherry on the silver tray between them and the two empty glasses, the rich savour of the wine in the room. Shelves filled with folders and envelopes bulging with papers.

'Pat, I know I can't.'

'Ah well, Mr Herbert, these are bad times for people with commitments and responsibilities. Like yourself. Me now, it's hard for me, too, but my needs are simpler and the demands on me nothing like those falling to yourself. There's always the lake of course.'

'What do you mean?'

For a moment Randall had a picture of the lake as a boating amenity, with picnics on the lawn in front of the picturesque oratory. Women in dinner dresses, gusted by the breeze. Steam launches.

'I mean,' said Scully, 'you can always throw yourself in.'

'Scully, spare me your wit. Look, would you like a little tot?'

Herbert moved towards the drinks cabinet and took up the whiskey decanter, relishing the feel of the smooth planes of cut glass in his hand.

'Too early for me, Mr Herbert.'

'Go on, just to be sociable.'

'A small one then, the smallest of balls of malt.'

Herbert poured the heavy amber liquid into two tumblers. They drank. Immediately Herbert felt the customary warmth invigorating his body. Down his lungs into his stomach, along the arms. He looked at Scully's face and admired his white hair and long, sorrowful nose. There was scarcely a man he knew that he did not find handsome. Now why was that?

Scully was speaking, but he'd missed the first few sentences. '... We need to make what adjustments we can, Mr H, and take the rough with the smooth. Let's hope they'll settle for the twenty-five.'

'Do you think they'll go for more? Another tot?'

'No, no more for me. I don't know. They'll go to their lords and masters for instructions. Your family is well enough thought of, but these days it's hard to tell. I'll be on my way, Mr H, I need to see the blacksmith about Nina's pony.'

He took his leave. Randall went over to the window, glass in hand. He leaned his forehead to the cool pane. Outside, the light had darkened slightly again. There was no one on the avenue or the lawn. The sycamores stirred faintly; a riot of tulips moved their red and yellow crowns. He began to talk to his dead father, aloud, saying that things had changed, that his architecture was now costing them dear. A slight sound made him turn round. His six-year-old daughter Nina was standing in the doorway, looking at him.

1918

MARY O'DWYER

She walked up French's Quay. She raised her eyes to look at the white stone of St Finbarre's Protestant Cathedral and saw the brass angel gleaming in the calm December sunlight. The air was clear and she was less tired than usual. Apart from those of her children who survived, there was Con's twin, who died at birth, and also three miscarriages. All those pregnancies in less than nine years. She had stopped him after Tom was born: that was six years ago now this month. All he had to do was look at her. At first she felt sorry for him, with that hangdog look he used to put on him in the early days, when he'd be lying next to her, pleading, whispering nonsense. But that was all over now. Now he was just sarcastic and bitter, that was whenever he threw her a word. He drank as many nights in the week as he could afford. He'd worked as a chauffeur for a while, and she didn't know for certain how he lost that good job with the Crosbies, but she had her suspicions. For the last couple of years he'd been driving for the bus company and getting good money, but every Saturday morning she had to drag out of him whatever he was prepared to give her. And now, on top of everything else, his sight was getting worse. In his half-sober moments, when he'd be feeling soft and self-pitying, he'd tell her that he was worried about the blur at the edge of his vision and that sometimes he was seeing double, and even occasionally he'd catch a glimpse of something that wasn't there at all. Mary thought that it might just be that he'd got himself blind drunk once too often; or perhaps he'd contracted some disease or other. She'd get the smell off him every now and then, the smell of perfume, and one or two of the neighbours – Mrs Lacey, for instance, or Freddie Crowley, the owner of the bread shop on Sullivan's Quay – would tell her, and not without a hint of pleasure, that he'd been seen in the Punchbowl, or the Laurel Bar, which is where you went if you wanted to pick up a jetty queen for the night.

She remembered how he was in the early days in Leeds, strong and slim and with thick black hair. His hair was still thick but it was now snow-white, over his blue eyes. He was kind then, but you'd never know, even at that time, when some fit of madness would take him and he'd be gone for days. And there was that business with the landlady. But when she recalled what he did for her in her time of trouble, and how he dismissed from his mind any concern about what anyone would say, she realised she still admired him as a man. And even though he betrayed her with that slut Liversedge in Leeds, he had come back, not with his tail between his legs, but grinning madly, standing in the doorway of Fat Mag's, his hand stretched out towards her, holding a wad of English money. He didn't know now what she was doing and she supposed it was possible that he would no longer care. She'd written to Morgan Holmes asking to see him and talk to him.

9 December 1918

Dear Mr Holmes,
I hope you will not mind me writing to you because I'm sure you have probably forgotten who I am, although I hope to God that you have not for your own sake as much as mine. I want to talk to you about my eldest son, Michael, and see what prospects there might be for him. He is now nearly fifteen, and he's a fine honest boy and I am proud of him, as I have every right to be. Please address any reply c/o Mrs Margaret O'Dwyer, The Viaduct, Rathcooney, Co. Cork.

Mary Condon (O'Dwyer)

She had taken Fat Mag into her confidence, who, in any case, knew the whole story from the start. And Fat Mag had agreed to Mary using her address. Even though Jim's sight was getting worse, he never missed the white rectangle on the floor of the hallway and always wanted to know what the letter contained. Sure enough, the reply from Morgan Holmes had come, asking her to come and see him at the stores.

She walked down past St Mary's of the Isle girls' school, then past the Sharman Crawford Institute, over the curving back of Clarke's Bridge. To the left there was a row of terraced houses, with a cinder track in front of them behind high railings, now gone shabby and covered with dust. Children played in the track in front of the long flights of steps. One, a girl of three or four, walked along the wall above the river. A small boy squatted in front of the railings, a basket beside him, containing branches of holly thick with berries. He held a branch up to her in his filthy hand and smiled at her through rotten teeth. 'Buy one for luck, missus. It'll bring you luck. Only a ha'penny.'

She took out the brown coin and gave it to him. He stood up and took a piece of newspaper from a sheaf he was sitting on and wrapped the bunch of holly for her, making a clumsy spray.

When she rounded the corner of the Maltings she could see Holmes's wholesalers before her just past the hospital. She got the smell of roasted barley from the Maltings, and its acrid tang reminded her of the many mornings she had walked along this quay towards work. The door was still painted its dusty duck-egg blue. She went up to the side office next to the big sliding doors and went in. The same clang off the bell as fifteen years ago. Morgan Holmes was standing over a secretary, examining a letter still in her typewriter. He looked up.

A physical shock ran through Mary's body. He was just as handsome as he had always been. He was wearing a suit of bird's-eye tweed, black and white, with a peaked collar, and a flowing blue tie. She noticed that his nails were smooth and rounded, and as he straightened up a coat sleeve rode up to reveal a generous cuff fastened with gold links. She looked at the long thin face with the severe but well-cut lips, the slight, trimmed moustache flecked with white, the remarkable eyebrows, and the brown hair and blue eyes. Standing where she was, on the other side of the counter, she got the male musky smell off him.

'Mr Holmes, I am Mrs Condon. I have an appointment to see you.'

When they were sitting down in his office, she handed him the bunch of holly. 'In memory of old times,' she said.

He took the poorly wrapped gift and laid it on his desk, alongside a model yacht with cloth sails and tiny ropes of twisted thread.

Around the office were photographs of himself and his wife at the regatta in Crosshaven, a holiday in some European city sitting outside a café drinking beer. Or there were pictures of old Mr Holmes at the golf club, or addressing a group of men at a dinner table.

'Happy Christmas, Mary. What can I do for you? But first, how are you?'

'I'm well. I keep myself to myself, Mr Holmes, as you know. I want to ask you a special favour which I think you are obliged to try to help me with. My husband is a useless drunk, and he's going blind. I have six children; the eldest of them is fifteen. And it's about him I wish to speak to you. He's ready to leave school and help out at home with some income. He's a good boy, and he'll work hard and loyally for anyone who'll treat him well. I'm asking you to give him a job. After all, he's your own son.'

Holmes breathed deeply, inhaling the green freshness of the holly, and looked at the crowded profusion of the berries amidst the bright glossy leaves.

1930

JACOB SLESS

Katherine Condon and her mother were walking up the Southern Road. The right-hand side of the steep hill was in shade, while the left, dwarfed by high mass-concrete walls surmounted with railings, was warm, made even warmer by the solid bulk of the concrete above them and the stone pavement beneath, which absorbed the still sunlight of this late April afternoon. Someone had been cutting a lawn in one of the gardens, which the high walls retained, and the smell of the shorn halms drifted down onto the warm street.

There were sounds of children laughing, which emphasised the quiet they walked through. A solitary man in a snowwhite shirt, sleeves rolled up, stood at the corner of Capwell Avenue and the Douglas Road. His arms were folded and he leaned back against the cast-iron window bars of the Southern Star, now officially shut until the evening trade, it being Sunday. As Katherine and her mother walked past they got the cool reek of porter from behind the closed doors. They could also hear the quiet murmurs of the illicit Sunday afternoon drinkers, obedient and grateful for the privilege of drinking in the dark, free of the horrors of family outings, walks, visiting relatives.

They walked past St Finbarr's Hospital, or The Union, as it was known in the city: it had served as a poorhouse, and had been used as a quarantine hospital during huge epidemics that wasted the city in Mary's mother's childhood and before. The place was dreaded.

Past The Union the road became even quieter, the houses larger. Semicircular frontages with recessed gates gave onto long avenues with red gravel, and above, behind trees, stood the houses, discreet, stable, ivy-cloaked. They turned into Elm Bank, Jacob Sless's residence, and walked up the wide curving avenue between dark rhododendron bushes. In front of the house, running along its full length, was a glass conservatory, where Katherine could see Mr Sless and his brother sitting in two cane armchairs.

Jacob greeted them and showed them into the conservatory, which was floored with sisal matting. They were drinking tea, and when Katherine and her mother entered, a broad-faced serving girl came out from the darkness of the house carrying extra cups, saucers and plates.

Katherine was a little surprised at herself and her mother. She had thought she would be overwhelmed by this experience, that her hands would shake, that she'd be tongue-tied, but nothing of this kind occurred. She took her cup and saucer from Jacob, which he gave to her with a little bow, in totally steady hands. She felt not a trace of discomfort: no prickly sensations of sweating, no butterflies in her stomach. With total assurance she carried the spoon, laden with white sugar, to her cup, and to her amusement she saw her mother delicately selecting a thin slice of lemon from a terracotta dish, and dropping it into her unmilked tea.

'Mrs Condon,' Jacob said, when the formalities were over, 'you have an excellent girl in Katherine; you should be proud of her.'

'Oh yes, Mr Sless. I certainly am.'

Katherine was relieved her mother didn't 'sir' Mr Sless, as she tended to do to those in authority. But Jacob was not someone whom you could comfortably call 'sir'. He was someone in whom fellow feeling was innate, and you knew that from his manner, his speech, his way of walking. And yet he had the reputation of being one of the richest men in Cork.

'How is Mr Condon? I gather he has not been too well these last years.'

'He's as well as can be expected,' Mary replied. 'He's stopped work now these eight years, and although his sight was good enough for him to do small repair jobs on cars up to a few years ago, he's almost totally blind these days. He can see blurred shapes when the light's good, and that's about all he can make out.'

She did not mention his now compulsive drinking, nor did the two brothers, who remained discreetly silent about something widely known all over the city. Jim Condon was headed towards self-destruction and his shabby figure could be seen in the doorways of pubs at ten thirty in the morning, waiting for them to open, 'his tongue hanging out', as Mrs Hennessy from the Marsh would say behind Katherine's back in the laundry. But there was no delight in his decline, as so often was the case. The Condon men were a mild and gentle breed, and seemed not to provoke hostility, even in a city where enmity was easily generated.

'It's a sad thing,' said Jacob, 'a sad thing.'

'I know your son Michael is very well thought of in Holmes's,' said Cecil. 'Mr Holmes was telling me the other day that he'd be lost without him. He's very reliable and trustworthy. And completely honest. What about your other children? Do you have other boys?'

'Well, yes, there's Con, who is working away now, thanks be to God; and Tom, who's still at school. Con is working on a cousin's farm out in Rathcooney.'

'Is he happy there?' asked Jacob.

'Well, yes, but it's very far out, and he has to stay over, which means he's sleeping in the barn most nights and washing at the pump in the yard.'

'Would he like a job here?' asked Cecil. 'We need a gardener.'

'He has no experience, Mr Sless.'

'Don't worry about that. I'll teach him. And he can have the little house at the bottom of the garden if he wants.'

Katherine thought this would be a godsend. The prospect of Con returning to the already-crowded home was something she did not wish to have to face. There would be all sorts of movements and adjustments to be made to accommodate another grown man back into the house.

'Come with us and we'll show you the garden,' said Cecil.

They went out on to the front lawn, now shaded by the tall oaks as the sun was going down. They walked round the side of the house into the large gardens at the back. Two girls were playing tennis on grass courts. Their hair was bobbed and they wore starched white outfits. Effortlessly they ran to each other's volleys, the white ball bounced softly on the green, then there was the soft report as the catgut connected with it, to send it away over the lightly swaying net at another angle. At the side of the court was a table with lemonade.

At the far end of the garden, beyond drills of freshly dug black earth, there was a small wooden house, with red curtains and a white door; the rest of the structure was of untreated wood. Katherine thought she would like to live there and bent down to pick a sprig of thyme.

Her mother reached out and took it from her. 'I love the smell of thyme,' she said.

1949

MICHAEL CONDON

I stood just inside the door between the hallway, my foot up on the chair kept in the alcove there, as I polished first one shoe then the other. I was careful not to get the polish on my socks. I'd pressed my own suit the night before. I didn't want to ask Ma to do it, she was in such a state. She'd never wanted any of us to marry. I remember she didn't speak to Katherine for weeks. She always had the same story: no one any of us had met or proposed to was good enough for us. It was funny with her — on all sorts of occasions, she would kowtow to people that she thought were important, and yet at other times she would think that we were above most others she'd come into contact with. Worst of all was the thought of parting with any of us. It was like a kind of death when we got married.

I looked at the crease in the trousers, which seemed sharp enough; the sleeves of the coat were ironed as well. A few days before I'd washed it in carbolic soap, taking care to soak the armpits and the crotch very thoroughly. Then plenty of cold water to sluice the suds out.

'You'll never get that bloody thing dry,' Ma had said, watching me ferociously from the corner between the oven and the coal hole. It was, in fact, a suit of clothes my father had bought some years before he died, when he was going to Leeds to a funeral. None of us knew where he got the money; and none of us knew who he was going to bury in Yorkshire. By then Ma wasn't talking to him at all, so he was left to sort himself out. He only had his pension for the blind, and must have found some way of borrowing or stealing the money for the suit. It was a good one, the white Cash's label on the inside pocket, with the name in black silk thread.

Tom, the youngest of the family, was to drive me to the church in my car. He was still single but going out with a girl down the road, so he was getting his share of abuse as well.

'There's the two of you,' Ma said. 'You there polishing your shoes like a gigolo, and you' – to Tom – 'dolling yourself up for that one from Friars' Avenue. Have neither of you any respect for yourselves, or for me, or for the Condon family? My heart is scalded with you. And it's not as if you are too young not to know what you're walking into. No. You're old enough, now, the pair of you, to know better. Marriage is only for those who can afford it, and you two are nowhere near well off enough to even think about signing your life away. For, and I'm telling you this now, and mark my words, when you sign that line later on this morning, Michael, you're signing away all your happiness. No marriage that I know of is a happy marriage unless there's pounds, shillings and pence. I suppose you'll say to me that you're going to live on love. Love doesn't put bread on the table nor meat in the pot.'

I tried to reply. I tried to call up what courage I had against this, but all I could think of were useless words that I knew would only increase her mockery and her contempt for me at that moment. I burned with shame. I bowed my head and blushed.

Tom spoke up: 'Will you catch yourself on, Ma. You've no right to speak to him like that this morning of all mornings, and he going out to be married to a woman he wants to spend his life with. Because you're bitter, you shouldn't trample on your son's happiness and hope.'

Tom was her favourite, even more than I, and she would take from him what she wouldn't take from anyone else. She was silenced.

'You were never happier,' he went on, 'than when Con went into the Cistercians in Mount Melleray; even though he'd left the job at Sless's, you were overjoyed. And why? Because you never wanted us to marry. And why that was, I don't know. Maybe someday I'll get to the bottom of it.'

She stood up, chin shaking, eyes flashing, her heart beating so fast I could see her chest thumping.

'How dare you. How dare you, you scut; hanging around with that fancy bitch down the road makes you think you can talk to me how you like. Well, I'll tell you this. There's none of you, none of you, good enough to lick the boots of my father and his stock from north Cork. And I don't know where this insolence has come from that you think you can talk to your mother this way. May Jesus Christ forgive you.'

'Ma,' I said weakly. 'Ma, he's only trying to make two halves of things. Come to the wedding. Couldn't you even come to the church for the sacrament, and say a prayer for me?'

'I'll say a prayer for you, all right. I'll pray that you will live to see the folly of what you've done. And that you won't be so worn out by children and work that you won't be dead in a few years' time. Because that's what's ahead of you all. Work and death.'

I still had one of my feet on the chair, a polishing brush in my hand. Suddenly something inside me collapsed, and my upper body fell onto my raised knee and I was crying like a child. I could hear my sisters moving around upstairs and was in dread that they would come down and find me in this state. 'Ma, Ma, please stop,' I said. 'You're destroying me, Ma. Have pity on me. Please. You know I would do anything for you, but please don't do this to me. I'll not marry her. I'll stop here. I'll not go. Tom, go down and tell Teresa I can't marry her.'

'What am I going to say? Michael won't marry you, Teresa, because his mother won't let him?' Tom shouted. 'Is that the message? Would you for God's sake, woman, catch yourself on. You're on the point of ruining your son's life.'

I could not stop crying. I was filled with pain and shame. I did not want to do anything, go anywhere, be anything any more. I wished I was dead and gone and out of this shouting.

Tom came up to me and put his arms around me. 'Michael,' he said, talking straight into my face. I could smell the bread he'd eaten for breakfast off his breath. 'Michael. Stop. Stop. Will you catch hold of yourself. You can't leave that poor girl down there.'

I turned and fell into the chair, putting my face into my hands and lowering them to my knees. Even in the middle of this distress I thought how strange it was that I was watching myself doing these actions. Like an actor. I was acting a part. And Ma was, and Tom, too. Bad parts, with a bad plot. I looked to the hallway and there, standing in the soft light from the frosted glass, I could see Ann and Sarah in their wedding finery, pale and awkward, holding their handbags and rosary beads.

'Pull yourself together,' said Tom.

I looked at him, my eyes scalding hot. I saw my mother crying as well. She was sitting near the stove, her blue overall up to her face, rocking herself as she cried, saying over and over: 'The lamb to the slaughter. The lamb to the slaughter.' Then she looked up, and said sternly: 'Out you go. You can't keep that girl waiting.'

I looked at her face, struck in stone. She seemed taller. My mind and stomach were a mass of tension and confused nerves. Her face, with its soft grey skin and prominent chin, the slight upward curve of the cheekbone under the eye, was now still, even relaxed.

'You'll have to go. No son of mine, it will ever be said, jilted a woman at the altar. No matter what she's like and no matter what the future holds for you, you've made that bed and you have to lie in it, come what may. Don't worry about me. I'll be all right here. I'll pray for you and for all of you that you may be kept safe in this terrible world.'

Tom pushed me out of the kitchen, through the hall door and down the concrete steps. I held on to the railing. The privet was in flower and I got the smell of its musky blossom. When last did I notice the smell of flowers? I was forty-five years old and I was getting married to Teresa Mulcahy from Kanturk.

1903

MORGAN HOLMES

He walked through the Luxembourg Gardens. It was a Sunday morning in April. The grass of the expansive parkland was still hung with a slight mist, an undulating wreath of white created by the sun's warm heat working on the dew that had fallen the night before. A family group preparing to have breakfast was sitting under a catalpa tree, its great oval leaves, still surviving from the previous summer, now a dark and reddish brown. Mother carefully wiped the moisture from a picnic table, while father snapped out portable, wooden-slatted seats. The girl was running around the tree kicking at the leaves, and the boy stood, looking into the cane food hamper.

A plate of hard-boiled eggs was produced, a small bottle of brandy, napkins spread, cold meat put out, and then a long baguette of crispy bread, which the father broke into four pieces. He then leaned down and placed two glasses on the table, into which he poured two small measures of brandy, which he and his wife drank down.

Morgan Holmes looked at this group and wondered what family life might be like. He had left Cork two days previously, arriving in Paris the day before. He walked through the gardens and then made his way to the Closerie des Lilas Café to where tables were being laid by a black-suited waiter: white linen folded between the cutlery, wine glasses, cruets of condiments and seasoning. Another waiter was brushing the terrazzo floor, and behind the bar stood a large lady, in a white blouse, eating bread and cheese. Holmes ordered white wine and bitters, then sat down in a dark corner. He lit a cigarette and blew the smoke over the green marble of his table, then drank deeply of the sweetish wine reddened by the tangy bitters. He thought of his father, sitting behind the heavy desk in his study, face dark, body inclined forward almost in an attitude of sorrow or prayer, speaking slowly.

'Morgan, you must tell me. Is this true?'

'I am afraid it is, Father.'

'And what are you going to do about it? What were you planning to do about it?'

'I don't know.'

'There's always . . . the option of, well, getting rid of it altogether.'

Morgan was shocked. He himself had, of course, thought of this as a way out, but found it deeply disturbing that his father should mention it. The older man went on, again speaking very deliberately, head cocked forward, looking at his hands spread on the desk before him, palms down.

'You'll understand that this remedy is one that I have no enthusiasm for. But the situation is desperate. You are in a completely exposed position. Could the girl be persuaded to

go to England? It might be possible to fix up suitable accommodation for her there, until her time comes, if she cannot be
enjoined to consider seriously the more drastic course of action.
There are ways and means.'

There was a long silence while Morgan watched a black cat
stretch itself outside the window on the sill, then arch its back
into what seemed an impossibly heightened curve.

His father began again, now rotating one thumb around the
other inside the small cage of his clasped hands. 'You know this
folly of yours has placed us in great jeopardy. We're depending
on the good opinion of the people of this town, and that's
something that can easily be withdrawn. In fact, they like to
do it when they can because they love nothing more than to
see people down. You seem not to realise that every step must
be a cautious one in the life we lead, and here you are, putting
all in danger, as well as yourself. What the hell were you
playing at, getting a young slip of a thing like Mary O'Dwyer
in the family way? At least you've not entertained any silly or
romantic notions.'

'Such as?'

'Marrying her, for one thing.'

'Actually, Father,' Morgan replied, 'I think that maybe that
is what I should do. She comes from a respectable family. I
know they're not well off, but she's been well educated, and
. . .' He broke off. He couldn't say what he was wishing
himself to say – that he loved her – because he did not know
if he did love her or not. He certainly did that night when they
first had sex out in the Black Ash, the train screaming by overhead as they lay behind the privet bushes of the viaduct, the
perfume of her body mixing with the sharp green smell of the
crushed leaves. He wanted to feel convinced, to be strong in his
resolution, but he found all traces of certainty ebbing away. He
felt nothing for her. Mary O'Dwyer. The name was just
sounds: no magic, no effect.

His father sensed his cowardice, his wavering, and realised
there was no danger. That Morgan would now be easily

tamed. Once cowed out of confidence, he'd never rebuild it

properly again. From that moment he knew that any feelings his son would ever have would be artificial, in that the damage he was now inflicting was deep enough to ensure that his son would never have sufficient daring to feel anything for anyone. This injury to Morgan meant that he could now use his son's impulses and divert him easily to his own purposes. He almost felt sorry for him. Raising his head, he looked steadfastly into his son's eyes, who lowered his gaze. Crestfallen.

'I think you need time to reflect, Morgan. Your actions have created a situation of great difficulty, and I think the best thing for you to do at the moment is to withdraw from it.' He couldn't resist a mocking jibe. 'Would that you'd done that before now!' His son blushed. It was apparent that he was a mass of confused, nervous agitation. Let him stew, his father thought. 'I want you to go away,' he said. 'Go to Paris for a few weeks. I'll try to sort this problem out with Mary O'Dwyer perhaps and her parents. I'll explore the various options. Meanwhile I want you to do the same with your own life. You've got certain things to resolve.'

The older man felt the thing he always experienced when he got someone to bow to his will. But then a fear assailed him: would Morgan be able for the job? Would he carry the firm? Would he be what he now showed no signs of being? Would he be ruthless and cruel, as required?

1847

PATSY CONDON

Patsy Condon and his wife had left the workhouse in Mitchelstown. The day before, Patsy, because he was related to Seamus Kearney, one of the overseers, got permission to break quarantine and had gone over to the women's sheds. Because of the widespread starvation and the epidemic, huge barns of rough planks had been built around the workhouse to accommodate the sick and the dying. The failure of the potato crop again this year had a completely demoralising effect. People everywhere were talking about the end of the world, the way Patsy remembered they used to yarn around the fireside when he was a boy, listening quietly to the talk –

stories spiked with a fear that he recalled as being like a cold black thing in his stomach. This same fear was now in everybody's face. People would arrive day after day at the workhouse and stand outside the walls, looking in through the gates. They envied those who were inside – envied their security, the fact that some food or other would be provided, in spite of the rumours going about that the Indian meal had been made lethal by the addition of rat poison. These crowds of people – old men, old women, families with batches of scraggy children – would stand silently outside the gates every day, and wait. Around noon, new admissions were made on the basis of the deaths the night before. Once the dead were logged, a corresponding number of admissions could be made. When the beadle came down to the lodge to tell the keeper the daily number there were screeches of entreaty as the crowd massed forward, arms outstretched, necks straining, veins swelling on temples, each trying to outdo the other. In the end it was a mixture of scramble and bribery, although handing the gatekeeper money in advance was no assurance, as he would more often than not forget he had agreed to see what he could do. It was necessary to push and shout, then to press money into his hand as he quickly counted the new inmates through, ten, fifteen, or whatever. Families were broken up, with children often badly maimed or even killed in the mêlée. It was all over very fast, a matter of seconds. After that day's hope and confusion were past, the crowd settled down again, peacefully. If the day were fine, there would be singing and occasional dancing, even though the weather was now beginning to enter the resolved bleakness of November. Prayers would be recited, a priest might turn up, or on some days there would be a visit from a group of local women, Protestant wives, who had prepared soup and bread for the children.

Patsy would look out at these women, from where he would stand, ten feet or so back from the gate, and watch their ministrations with a remote and baffled wonder. He'd watch one of them roll up a sleeve of black calico and he'd note the

greyish skin of the arm, the soft hands, the silence between the
ladies as they went on with their charitable work. Their dresses
clacked and rustled as they moved, the cloth heavy about their
limbs. But his gaze kept being drawn back to their faces, cold
and grey in the November light. Their confidence and energy
made him afraid, but he found it hard not to continue looking,
as at some rare and bizarre species.

He had wanted to see Celia again, and hoped she'd agree
with what he wanted to do. Kearney had been difficult to
persuade, but Patsy gave him one of his remaining shillings,
and was allowed permission to visit the women's enclosure
within the compound, under strict supervision. Celia had
agreed to his proposal that they leave the workhouse, where
there was nothing before them only a lonely death apart from
each other. Better anything than that, she thought.

They were now climbing a hill. It was frosty and late. They
had had nothing to eat all day, except for a raw turnip Patsy
had stolen from the workhouse that morning before they left.
People had stood at the gateway to watch them go; a handful
had been given permission to see them to the entrance. There
was puzzlement as to why they should want to leave: how
could they face out into that desert, that derelict country? But
Patsy was resolved. He was being led by some instinct inside
him, something dignified. He did not want to stay there,
locked in, to end up like a lunatic or a beast driven mad.

They had now reached the top of the hill. Below them the
valley shone in the moonlight. Celia was exhausted and was
walking with her arm thrown about his shoulder for assistance,
panting after the exertion of the climb.

'We'll rest soon,' he said, 'once we find a place to lay our
heads that'll be snug and dry even if there's nowhere warm on
a night like this.'

He looked up at the stars, and saw Orion's belt and the
Pleiades, all blue and orange and white.

She looked up, too, into the silence. 'God is good and His
ways are not ours,' she said.

They walked on. There ahead, beside the road, the hiss and gurgle of a stream. Even though it was very cold, they were thirsty. They came to where the stream went under the road in a culvert, and at the bottom of the embankment there was a small pool, silver in the thin light. They scrambled down and drank greedily, lifting their mouths to look at each other. He watched the water fall off her face in shining thin rivulets, then drop back into the now ruffled surface of the pool. They laughed.

Some distance away from the road was a cabin on which the thatch was still intact.

'Let's go there,' he said.

They pushed open the door. There was a scurry of vermin on the floor, but they could see the place was reasonably dry in the light from the doorway and the curtainless windows. There was still some kindling in the hearth and Patsy found a few armfuls of turf in the lean-to shed outside. He lit a fire. As he knelt down over the flames he looked sideways at Celia and saw her long face, white and thin, the dignified nose, the elegant lips. Her body, despite her having carried four children, was still slim. He thought of the four graves around their own house, one for each of their children, all dead in seven days. Even that didn't break her spirit, but he didn't know what he was doing for days, so when she had suggested the workhouse he'd gone along with her. It seemed to offer some hope.

The fire was warming them a little and she now sat in front of it, her hands around her knees. When her skirt fell back he saw, in terror, that her ankles had swollen up to twice their size. She had it, the fever.

'My legs are cold, Patsy.'

He moved towards her and pulled her feet to his chest and stomach. They were freezing.

'Don't mind them. Just go to sleep.'

She closed her eyes in his warmth, and quickly her breathing grew deep and regular. She stirred and he moved alongside her so that her head rested on his shoulder. He did not stir for fear he'd awaken her, and even when the fire died down he did not build it up again. He continued to hold her to him. Her breathing became very slow and faint and then stopped altogether. He stayed with her like that until the morning.

When the sun came up he laid her down and went out for the turf-cutter's *sleán* he'd seen the night before in the lean-to. Already the dogs had gathered, four or five of them, and when he lunged at them with the *sleán* they didn't even bark. They just moved back slightly. He'd make the grave as deep as he could.

1935

KATHERINE CONDON

I remember the first mornings after we'd got back from the Shelbourne Hotel in Dublin. It was bitterly cold and still Tim would go out to the tap in the back yard to wash in the open air. He liked the cold water; he said it cooled his blood. It needed cooling, no doubt about that. I'd stand at the range and put on the two rashers and have the eggs to one side, ready to put on when the bacon was half done. I could see him standing in the cold air, taking deep lungfuls of it, his breath white in the sharp frost. It would still be quite dark, so his stomach and shoulders stood out clearly in the brightening air, blue turning to faint gold. He shuddered and chattered out burring sounds as he splashed the freezing water all over his upper body, then taking the yellow soap, he lathered himself under the arms, between his legs and behind. He then dipped his head and sluiced the water through his brown hair, which fell in front of his eyes, a short, even curtain. He soaped that, and then, taking an old saucepan, rinsed his entire body, beginning with his hair. He came naked into the kitchen, and stood in front of the old black range, which was now sending out pulses of dry heat. He took the warmed cloth from the rack hanging over the stove and towelled himself, looking at me, laughing. 'Do you want a quick one now, sunny-side up, while the eggs are frying?'

He said 'sunny-side up' with an American accent, mockingly imitated from the pictures.

'Get your clothes on, you – have not you enough of it at night-time without wanting it at all hours of the day?'

I was surprised at his urgency and insatiable need. When we lay in bed together, before starting, he would tremble with excitment. This was all new to me. I had no experience of a man before getting married. The usual glauming and shoving at dances. Once there was a fellow in the Arcadia who said he was from Cavan, and when I pushed him away, after he'd been trying to ram himself against me, he said: 'Look girl, have pity on me. If you don't give me a hand with this thing here in my trousers, it'll eat the leg off me.'

I felt then I should hit that fellow a slap across the face, but as he said it he closed his eyes in a mock agony, then pretended to swoon and half fell on top of me. All I could do was laugh.

'Is that how you lot court up in, where is it, Virginia? The place you come from is not well-named, if you're anything to go by. You should be ashamed of yourself to talk like that.'

'Don't blame me, girl. It's that bloody thing that's snaking around my leg this minute and if he doesn't get a look at yourself, he'll have half my thigh chewed away. He's a beast, I'm telling you, and there's no controlling him.'

She remembered his short curly black hair and the strange

lively burr in the voice: the North.

The rashers were done. Tim was pulling on the woollen socks I'd darned the night before, waiting for him to come in from the late shift. He'd come home at half past twelve, having cycled up from the factory down the Marina. I watched him, the compact, stocky body of him, the big hands and thick fingers that could be so gentle, and I felt safe. A man. He was a ball of energy. He was going back into work again at four o'clock in the afternoon, but now he was cycling off to Blackrock, where he was building a garden shed for someone.

He poured us out two cups of tea while I toasted bread at the reddened grille of the range, the lower coals now burning brightly. We sat down to eat. In the silence I watched him cut his toast into strips which he sank into the egg yolk, then eat the yellowed toast with bits of bacon, parted from the big, thickly cut rashers.

'That'll keep the heat in you until dinner time. You'll get something out in Blackrock?'

'I will – she's a decent sort. A lady. Like you.'

He looked at me and happiness drove through me like a wave of electricity when I saw his frank and open face, his clear eyes, strong hands.

We left the house together – he on his bike to Blackrock, I down to the laundry on the South Main Street. Before he set off, he leaned over on his bike, one foot on the pathway, to kiss me. I smelt the clean smell of his yellow washing soap.

I walked along Langford Row and up Douglas Street, the same direction I used to take when I was going to school in the convent. This was a Thursday, so we were coming to the end of our first week of living together. The end of last week had been spent in Dublin at the hotel.

I'd been the first to get married out of the house. Ma nearly had a seizure when I told her I was getting engaged to Tim Harding. I had made sure I got him into the house once or twice, and she'd been polite enough, in a chilly way. He had a good job, and men with good jobs were hard to find. He dressed well, quite carefully, and he had a well-bred way of standing still and only saying what he had to say, going no further. All of these things Ma took in, but nothing prepared us for the outburst when I made the announcement. It was late Saturday night about eleven o'clock. Michael was ensconced in the chair by the door, Sarah and Ann were gossiping as they disentangled a large yarn of knitting wool, and Tom was reading a comic by the fire. Da was out, raising the elbow, as ever. There was a peaceful atmosphere when I came in. I'd left Tim at the top of the steps, and my heart was light with pleasure. He had pressed me to tell Ma, and offered to come in with me, but I said I wanted to do it myself. I was pleased at my decision to tell her, and trusted that she'd be happy for me.

She was talking to Michael. 'Be sure you ask Mr Holmes if he could let us have some bacon offcuts for next weekend, and Katherine' – turning to me – 'would you ask Mr Sless, who we know has a soft spot for this family, to let us have some seasoned onions? Isn't it a fine thing that you have a decent employer to look after you?'

I always liked being praised by Ma. It seemed a good moment. I said the words I'd gone over in my head a million times: 'Ma, Tim has asked me to marry him and I've said I will.'

She was standing at the sink. With a sudden convulsive movement, she caught hold of a plate from the wooden drainer and flung it at me. I was so surprised I had no time to duck and it hit me on the shoulder, hard.

She shouted, 'Jesus Christ Almighty – what are you saying? Are you out of your mind? Who is that bastard anyway? What do you know of him? You can do better than that bloody dandy. May God and His Blessed Mother give you sense. Do you want to make a desolation of your life?'

I tried hard to stop myself screaming back at her. She was already hoarse and Sarah broke in, in the gap caused by her voice breaking down.

'Look, Ma,' she said. 'Don't be getting upset. I'm sure we'll sort all of this out.'

'There's no sorting out. Let her get to hell out of here with her fancy man. I'll have no more to do with her or him. I'll not speak to her again until I hear from her own lips that she has given up this stupid notion.'

'Ma,' I said. 'Ma, please try to understand that you're ruining my happiness.'

'She doesn't seem to realise what I've said,' Ma said to Michael and to Tom, deliberately not looking at me. 'I'm not talking to her until she comes to her senses.'

We all then knew for the first time how Ma hated any of us marrying. She didn't speak to me until just before the wedding, which Tim and I arranged in six weeks, so that people were talking. We didn't care. We felt strong.

1903

MARY O'DWYER

She climbed the stairs to Elliott Holmes's office. The walls were painted what her mother would call 'biliousy green', and shone in the dull afternoon light. She'd had a light lunch over in Winthrop Street in a new café in the arcade with Jim Condon, a driver with the Cork Steam Packet Company. The lunch of cold potato salad and corned beef with Vienna bread was lying surprisingly light in her stomach. So often now she brought up anything she ate in less than an hour. She was getting thinner: people were saying that she was losing weight. As yet there wasn't even the slightest hint of an incriminating bulge beneath her stays. Her face, instead of growing plumper and softer, which she thought would happen, had developed a finer tone and edge. The skin was paler and her cheekbones more pronounced. She knocked on the frosted glass of the door.

Elliott Holmes came to greet her and ushered her to a chair. A chill air was blowing into the room from the window which was slightly open. Old Mr Holmes was famous for his fondness for fresh air, even in midwinter. This was March, and the wind was sharp. He wore a heavy tweed suit, with a loud waistcoat, and a fob chain. He smelt of tobacco and money. She was scared. She felt again something that had started to infiltrate her feelings ever since she knew she was pregnant by Morgan Holmes, that she and her like were totally vulnerable, and that Holmes and his people were entirely powerful. That was why they gave off this spice of energy, why they moved with such bustle even when they got older. She had resolved in her mind not to be like her mother, quailing before every new experience, wondering if the next person she had to meet was to her advantage or not. But now she wasn't too sure if she was going to be able to hold to this. She was frightened of the capacity life had to hurt, and of her own readiness to accept the injuries inflicted. She felt her courage had gone very low. She'd asked Morgan what he wanted to do about their situation, and the memory of his baffled face, so like the one before her with its sharp blue eyes and dark brown hair, came back to her. He'd said he loved her, but he didn't know how it could be sorted out. She remembered how he had promised her that he would be faithful and protect her, that he'd said, that night out in the Black Ash as the train thundered overhead, that he would die for her if need be. She'd laughed then, full of delight at his extremity; but she never thought that it might be she who would die for him, and for his father with those selfsame cold, blue eyes.

'Mary,' Holmes began, 'I would like you to have a sherry before we begin. We have an intractable subject before us that will take all our best endeavours to –'

'No thank you,' said Mary. 'I don't drink, Mr Holmes.'

She was trying to hold herself steady and alert. This old man was a fox and she knew Morgan was frightened of his cleverness and power.

'You won't mind if I do.'

In deliberate silence he carefully poured himself a glass of pale sherry in a long thin fluted glass. The cold air of the room was immediately suffused with the sharp sweet smell of the sherry. He drank. 'Fine dry Amontillado,' he said.

Languidly he drifted back to the desk and sat behind it, placing the glass on a silver coaster and looking past her at the door. He leaned back in the chair, flexing his back slightly so a bone or two cracked in his spine. Then he stretched his legs out underneath the desk.

'I'm aware of your delicate condition,' he said, and stopped. Silence for seconds.

'I'm sorry, Mr Holmes?'

'I know that you claim that my son has made you pregnant.'

It was like getting a violent blow on the cheek. Tears started into her eyes. Be calm, she said to herself. 'I don't know what Morgan may have said to you, Mr Holmes, but I do not claim anything. I'm saying what is true, and I've said it to no one else. Your son has made me pregnant, and offered to marry me.'

'No one can be sure who's the father of a child; even the mother herself can't be sure at times.'

She could scarcely reply. 'I don't know what you're implying,' she said. 'No man ever touched me apart from Morgan. And for you now to say this is very unfair.'

She knew she was appealing to a hopelessly distant God to whom she was an irritating insect to be cleared away. And how could it be otherwise?

'I mean no disrespect to you, of course, but if, I stress *if*, my son has been indiscreet he has not been so on his own. It takes two to do what you have done.'

He now allowed himself a salacious smile, hoping to engage

her complicity. But no, she stayed firm. She didn't smile back.

'Please help me,' she said, and immediately regretted it. But what choice do I have? she asked herself. She went on: 'I haven't seen Morgan in days. Where is he?'

'Paris,' replied Holmes. 'He went to Paris to get away from things for a while. He's under a lot of strain and he's not used to coping with problems. Between ourselves, Mary, he's had an easy life, and it's made him, what shall I say, thoughtless. He doesn't really think about the consequences of what he does. He's always surprised at outcomes, even when he should know exactly what he's let himself in for. He's a little weak.'

Paris. He'd gone to Paris and left her to the mercies of this bony lizard. She looked at the blue eyes under the prominent eyebrows. Nothing still, just appraisal. 'Why did you ask to see me?' she said.

'I thought,' he sighed, 'that I should place before you certain options. One will relieve you of all the problems consequent on both your actions; the other will allow you to manage them better.'

'Please tell me out straight what you're thinking of.'

'There is the possibility, the real possibility, of removing the problem altogether. I have a good surgeon friend on Patrick's Hill who can, in very special circumstances, be persuaded to perform a most delicate operation.'

'You want the baby killed.'

'No, no, my dear; no, no. This is an option I'm talking about, in which the foetus is removed before it, well, you know, before it causes any trouble.'

'I'm not a well-educated person, Mr Holmes, but that is not how I see it. It is not an option.'

'The other is that you go to England, and have the child there, and have it adopted by your Church's authorities. I can fix up a place in Leeds.'

'Your son did promise marriage, Mr Holmes.'

'That, my dear girl, is not an option.'

1903

MORGAN HOLMES

Morgan Holmes was lying stretched out on an Aubusson carpet. The curtains were drawn on the Paris evening. He was on the flat of his back looking at the ceiling where the plaster cornices were alive with marble arabesques. Slim girls fled from bearded men with huge phalluses. To the side of his head there was a long-stemmed pipe and an ashtray. A Chineseman ushered in the girl he'd asked for, a tall Eurasian. She stood above him, flexing a naked leg through her split dress. The pain arrived through the opium cloud and he accepted it gratefully.

1847

PATSY CONDON

It was late morning by the time Patsy Condon reached the road leading up to his house outside Glenduff in the Kilworth Mountains. There were very few people left in the village itself. The drinking house was closed up and shuttered, the row of cabins along the street were empty, too, but there had been no attempt to protect them against intruders. The doors of most of them stood open, the windows smashed, and already damp had begun to make the thatch sag in large clumps hanging down in the dark interiors. There was the smell of wet from the charred remains of fires in the hearths, rain having flowed down the cold chimneys.

In a doorway stood a young girl, aged about five, in a blue nightshirt. Her hair was caked in grime, and her lips were blackened with filth. She sucked her thumb and looked at him.

He spoke to her. 'Where are your mammy and daddy?'

'I don't know, sir; they were here yesterday but today I can't find them.'

'Where are you from?'

'I'm from up the Funchion river, in the Ballyhoura hills,' she said, in a kind of sing-song.

'When did you get here?'

'Yesterday.'

'Have you brothers and sisters?'

'I have, sir, two brothers and a sister.'

'And did you all come together?'

'We did, sir. We had to leave. And the master was very kind to my father. He gave him two shillings for the road. More, my daddy says, than many of our kind have.'

'And what is your kind?'

'Our kind, my daddy says, are the people who are not there.'

'And you don't know where your people have gone?'

'I don't know, sir. They were here last night and they have now gone. My small brother, Tomeen, was very sick and I think my mother wanted to take him somewhere where he could get well. They always said I was the strongest and they wouldn't carry me when I was tired because there was always another one who was more tired than me.'

'Will you come with me, little girl? I'll carry you.'

'I'm not tired, sir, but I think I should wait awhile. They'll be back.'

'They may have to go a long way to find someone to help your brother, child. I have to do something in my house up the road. When I come back along this way again we'll see if they have come. If they haven't I think maybe you'd better come along with me. Do you know where I'm going?'

'Where?' she asked, looking closely at him, her thumb still in her mouth.

'America.'

'Oh.' She said no more, just kept on looking up at him.

'I'll be going on.'

As he walked past the small huxter's shop he saw O'Mahony's pale face inside the window, looking out at him, the curtain pulled aside. The head, bald as an egg, stared at him, following him as he went by, and made no gesture of recognition. Patsy's eyes salted up, but he took a deep breath and walked on; resolving in his heart never to forget this bitterness. His hurt and anger calmed him, as he buried it away deep in his mind, a reservoir of dark to be called upon, as needed.

When he got to the house, apart from others on a green hilltop, the roof had been beaten in. Laths and straw, mixed together, hung down, as he could see through the gaping hole where the doorframe had stood. The four graves, dug at the four points of the compass, the youngest at the northern point, still had their small cairns of stones intact, and the four wooden crosses were upright. He stood and bowed his head at each in turn, and prayed for the peace of their souls, and for that of his wife, now with them, looking after them again, as he wished himself to be.

He went inside and found the dresser broken, and cups and plates strewn about the floor. He walked into the room behind the fire and saw that the clothes' chest had gone, but some of the clothes had been thrown around, probably thought not worth taking. Spreading out an old sheet he gathered them up; then, knowing that never again would he set foot in this house, he went over to the corner and having taken an iron from the side of the fire, lifted with difficulty the large corner flagstone off the smooth sandy earth where it lay. There, he found his last resource, the gold coin his mother had given him for luck when he built this cabin with his own hands fifteen years ago. She'd told him to touch it only as a last resort. It was to keep the luck in the stones of the house, so that even when he'd left for the workhouse with Celia he'd not lifted it, hoping, somehow, he'd find a way of coming back. But now this was the end.

He climbed into the loft, and found, safely wrapped in oiled cloth where he'd left it, the fiddle he'd bought in Mitchelstown fair from a Clare tinker. He always thought it a lovely thing, even though it had been made from bits and pieces of sea wrack, and oak from the bottom of a sherry cask. The wood was shaved fine, and the bridge of the instrument gleamed with a polished lustre from many applications of boiled linseed oil. Standing on the boards of the loft, he resined the thick-haired bow, and played a few bars of a slow air, 'The Mermaid'. The house filled with the sound.

He came downstairs, put the fiddle carefully into the bundle. He gave the door of the dresser a fierce kick, driving in the timbers, then left.

The child was standing where he'd left her an hour or so before. O'Mahony looked out at him from behind his curtain as Patsy went up to her.

'They haven't come?' he asked her.

'No, sir. I don't know what to do, sir. You're going to America?'

'To America, yes. Will you come with me? I'll look after you, I promise, and I'll never leave you behind me anywhere.'

'I'll go with you, sir.'

She walked up and put her slight hand into his, keeping the thumb of her left hand in her mouth. 'Will we have adventures, and will you carry me when I'm tired?' she said.

'Yes we will, child, and I'll carry you everywhere.'

Again Patsy's eyes salted up. He looked through the blur across the street at O'Mahony's face, which was grinning, as much as to say: you've been caught.

They took the road to Queenstown, hand in hand, and were in Cork in a day. From there they went on to the Great Island in Cork harbour and then to Queenstown.

1903

JIM CONDON

He swung the tram round the long corner at the bottom of the Headrow in Leeds. He looked at the main street, lit on both sides by gas lamps, and saw the pavements crowded with people, darkly dressed, coming out of offices, and making their way home through the murk and smog. He still liked the rancid smell of this city, even though he'd picked up, in casual conversations in pubs in Headingley and in Hyde Park, that the air was poor in Leeds, and that it caused ill-health. But he relished the dark fume, laden with factory smells and coal smoke: it had a tang of iron and copper in it, the bite of metal, furnaces, hot steel. He looked at the tramlines in front of him, as he drove the vehicle swiftly down towards Leeds Parish Church, his next halt. The steel parallels shone blackly in the gaslight and remaining daylight, and he thought how they would have been, not long ago, a crimson rivulet poured into a wet mould, then slowly stiffening as the steam arose from the water ladled on, the whole operation giving off the smells of the earth.

Six weeks in Leeds. He stopped at the church, and the passengers climbed on. He liked the way they called each other 'love', irrespective of sex. These were a mixture of clerks, secretaries, office girls in long dresses, market workers, carrying jute bags of vegetables and fruit, all headed for Hunslet and Beeston, where there were streets after streets of tiny back-to-back red-bricked houses with cobbled back lanes, neat yards, and a little wash house in each one.

He'd got a job driving with the Leeds Tramway Company almost immediately after making contact with some friends up the York Road, originally from the Mitchelstown–Fermoy area and now active in the trade union movement in Leeds. One of them, Fergal O'Dowd, had been in the Fenians a long time ago. Jim told himself that he cared little for politics – let that to the talkers and arguers, he'd say – as long as he had enough in his pocket for his keep and a few pints of a night. He thought of himself as easy-going, and he was careful never to run or to hurry anywhere. He hated when somebody called after him, or shouted at him. It was an indignity. That was why he liked driving and was good at it. Driving allowed you to get from place to place while taking your ease. He was methodical, careful, steady, deliberate; and always thought ahead about what was required. He liked visiting factories, seeing people working well: it satisfied in him that instinct which associated thoroughness with dignity, reliability with care. He was happy enough to agree with anyone as long as it didn't put him out too much. He was conscious that he had a kind of style, and he noticed that others were aware of it too. Woman looked after him in the street, drawn by something, which he felt might be related to his not getting flustered, letting things be. Machines and he seemed to have a special understanding: they nearly always did what he wanted them to do, and if a problem did arise, his hands would go almost instinctively to the tappet, spring, conduit, or switchgear that was causing the breakdown in the system.

He was in Leeds because Mary O'Dwyer needed him to take her. The day they had lunch together in the Winthrop Arcade, he had to take Simmons, the visiting director from Liverpool, to the fishing inn he always stayed in out in Carrigrohane. He was driving back to his flat in Sheares' Street when he saw Mary crossing the road by the Maltings. He'd met her a few times when he'd been collecting old Holmes to take him to lunch at the Cork and County Club. He blew the horn at her and its raucous sound made her turn around, as well as drawing the attention of all the other pedestrians. It was a cold day and he was muffled up and wearing goggles while driving, so she didn't recognise him at first. He waved her over, pulling up outside St Francis Hall and as he did so he removed his scarf and slipped the goggles up on his forehead. Mary stood on the kerbstone, looking up at him, sitting high above the tiny wheel that he still held with one gloved hand. The engine snorted and growled, then spluttered into silence.

'Will you come for a spin?' he asked.

'No. Thank you. I don't feel like it.'

She looked down the street, away from him, towards the courthouse. It was getting dark. He saw she was pale. A gust of wind blew the green scarf sideways from her face, and he noticed the red tints in her light brown hair.

'I've had a shock,' she said.

'Look, I'll put this away and we'll have a chat. Walk down after me.'

He got down and started up the motor again, turning the cranking handle, and the thing broke into shuddering and noisy life. He drove it down Sheares' Street and into the close behind the Academy Dairy, where he steered it into the dry

hay barn at the back. She was standing under the archway of
the alley leading into the yard when he came out. They walked
together down to the Raven, where they sat in the snug inside
the green-painted window with its frosted glass.

'What's happened?'

'I can't tell you but thank you for being so kind. I can't tell
anyone. I don't know what to do.'

'You'll have to tell someone. Why not me?'

'I don't know you. We've met a few times, and we've had
lunch today. That's all.'

'All right, so. Will you come out with me tonight?'

'Where to?'

'We can go to the Opera House. And before that, I'll take
you to the Tivoli.'

'You must be rolling.'

'A driver is a well-paid job. There's very few who can drive
safely. But it's the way everyone will travel in the future. For
the time being drivers are sure of a good wage.'

During the interval at the Opera House they were sitting in
the bar, she drinking lemonade, he having his third pint of
stout of the evening, when he said: 'Look, I'm bored with all
this highfalutin Shakespeare stuff. I prefer a variety act myself,
or the clowns, or jugglers. Let's go back to the Raven.'

She didn't know what her mother would say when she got
back. She had never gone out straight from work without
telling them at home what she was doing. She felt fearful and
yet oddly reckless and excited as well. 'All right,' she said. 'And
when we get there I want a dirty big glass of porter.'

In the Raven she took her first drink of stout, her first real
taste of alcohol apart from minute sippings of sherry allowed to
her at Christmas as a child. It tasted rank and foul and acrid, but
it left a lingering on the tongue and in the back of her throat
that drove her to take another drink. This time her whole head
filled with the taste, as a warm slightly numbing peace settled
slowly on her mind.

'Jim,' she said, 'I'm in trouble.'

'What kind of trouble?'

'The worst that can happen to a woman.'

He put his hand out to hers under the circular wooden table and held it. It was warm and a little damp. In the main body of the pub, which had now filled up, there were the riotous bleatings and roars of drunken men. In the corner of the snug an old woman sat, head covered in a black shawl, whimpering to herself, a smoking hot whiskey in front of her. They were alone apart from her, and she was taking no notice.

'Kiss me,' Mary said.

He leaned over the table and put his lips to hers. They were soft and strange. A wildness arose in him.

'Who's the bastard's done this to you?'

'I won't say.'

'What's he going to do about it?'

'His father tried to talk me into having it done away with and when I wouldn't agree to that he said he'd fix me up with a place in Leeds.'

'Leeds? I know people in Leeds. There's no way you're going there alone. I'm coming with you.'

'What? I don't even know you.'

'Look what the people you know have done to you. What's he going to offer you? Where is the bastard? Why are you talking to his father?'

'It's too complicated.'

'Tomorrow you go to whoever it is and get what you can out of them; then we'll go to Leeds and see what this place is they want to fix you up with. We'll go. Tomorrow.'

'Tomorrow? Don't be stupid. What about your job?'

'I'll get one there. Don't worry. Let's just go. A driver can always find work. And stay the night with me. Don't go home.'

'I can't do that.'

'Why not?'

As Jim drove the tram down towards Hunslet, its single light now a solid beam in the dark, lighting up the silvery tracks of the lines, he got the smell of the hay in the barn at the back of the dairy where he and Mary had laid down for an hour that night before he took her up to his flat. There he made her a cup of tea and they went to bed together, laughing.

1625

GEOFFREY KEATING

Looking out from my window this fine spring day I can see
the main road between Dublin and Cork way below me, a thin
white straggle in the sunshine. It is still too early for the
highway to be very busy, but there are some specks of movement: a cart with a man leading the animal by a halter, slowly
walking northwards towards Cahir; a woman with a bundle of
kindling on her head, dressed in a crimson cloak. Around her
the May blossom will be exhaling its milky smell. I've been
alone now for weeks, living off the dried meat and flour
brought to me. I have a tiny cabin up here, on the side of
Galteemore, set in a little wooded enclosure, behind neat stone

walls, with a clear view of the path all the way down. No one will come near here without my seeing them first. I'm ready for anyone.

I look to my left: the nearest house miles away is Muircheartach Ó Condúin's farmhouse, where he lives with his family – a wife and nine children. He is my protector, my chieftain, my lord, as I tell him grandiosely whenever he comes. This amuses him, my attempt to renovate, in mockery, the old ways. The last time he was here with the supplies he said: 'You must be missing the attention of women and the recognition of the scholars up here.'

'Not at all,' I replied. 'I'm glad to be out of all that strife and effort. The recognition of scholars is never given, always coerced, by force. Don't you know that?'

'No, no. Surely not. Isn't there a confederacy of learning, a consistory of the blessed, and a fraternity of knowledge?'

'Scholars pretend to these gentilities, but in reality the greatest brigand who ever lived hardly outdoes them in rapacity, greed and anger. The scholar's sin, Murty, is envy, the worst of all the passions. The worst.'

'Worse than lust? That's a strange theology.'

'Maybe. But in France these things are accepted more readily. When I was in Rheims I remember the Bishop saying to me, one day as we walked in the square in front of the cathedral, just before we took our dinner, that the Irish paid too much attention to sex. "They have," he said, "a reputation for concupiscence and amorousness from as long back as anyone can remember. Here in Rheims we say that that was why their famous Eriugena decamped from the native sod. An obsession with the genitalia. That is still the lore in Rheims about your adopted country and the town believes it comes from Eriugena's own words when he turned up here a thousand years ago." That was what, Murty, the Bishop said, and I think he's right. We're obsessed by fornication, whether our own or other people's, such that all the other vices have a field day, liberated by this one-eyed preoccupation.'

Murty laughed. 'You yourself can't absolve yourself from the vice of lust. Everybody knows that thing you wrote asking the lady to stop, to take away her hand, which as a piece of filth is as good as any bardic bawdiness, especially from the likes of yourself with all that English blood in you.'

'I never admitted to that scurrilous piece of filth, as you call it.'

He was talking about a poem I'd written while a divinity student at Bordeaux, after a night out on the town, full of Gascony wine, a piece which one of my friends had taken back to Ireland with him, where it had become a favourite piece of mock-heroic recitation, first among clerics at drinking parties, then spreading more widely, all the more attractive because of its having been written by a lovesick priest asking a girl to stop tormenting him. It's followed me ever since.

'You may not have admitted to it, but do you, Father Keating, now formally deny the authorship of that obscene document?'

'Ah look, Murty,' I said, 'leave me alone, will you? The reason why I value so much this peace and quiet is because I have time to reflect and to prepare myself for the task ahead.'

'I know,' said Murty. 'God's winds blow much towards us, good mixed with ill in the blast.'

He put down the bags of flour and dried meat on the scrubbed table, and went out the door and down the hill, stopping on the path just above the declivity in the copse below to wave and smile. My protector in my time of need.

I've been in hiding for years now, pursued by the wrath of the man whose authority I provoked by naming, from the public altar, his mistress and he. A vile, arrogant scut called Blennerhassett, rolling in an adulterous bed with the fat wife of a burger of Cashel. I don't know what came over me: one of those invasions of rage which afflict me from time to time. I was giving a sermon on, of all things, the body of Christ as experienced by us physically in the Mass under the aspect of bread, when I launched into an extempore effusion on truth,

and how the true body of Christ could not be gainsaid by our
actions, however covert we may think them to be. I ranted on
about the falseness of privacy, that everything stood naked
before the Lord; that the soul, wracked by remorse, could find
no hiding place when all was made plain and clear in death.
Then I saw her fat, composed and sanctimonious puss down
in front of me, lips pursed in the simulacrum of pious medita-
tion, and I felt something, a clot of hate, explode in my head.
Then I was off accusing directly, rebuking, shouting. There was
a shocked silence when I finished, and when I started into the
Creed no one rose for a minute or more.

Her nibs got up, in a flounce of satin and an audible creaking
of stays, and standing ashen-faced before me, spoke: 'You'll
regret the day you did this.'

She traipsed out, her children streeling behind her, a jostle of
navies, and pinks, and whites. I turned and walked back into
the sacristy, saying to the congregation as I went that there
would be no Mass that day and publicly asking God to forgive
me. Since then Blennerhassett has been attempting to have me
arrested on the grounds of defamation, but I've kept myself
safe, moving from one place to another and preparing myself
for the task which I have set myself as a penance for this great
sin of mine and for all my other offences. I thank God for that
fall from grace, because without it I would never have had the
resolve to undertake what I am about to undertake.

And what I am about to undertake, in expiation of my fault,
frightens me so much that sometimes I sit in front of the pages
of blank paper poised to write, but sweating, my heart beating
fast, my writing hand trembling. I think perhaps no one ever
undertakes a work that he knows may defeat his abilities unless
he has something to atone for. I know what I must atone for.
That blackness in my life, that lethargy of heart, which created
the slough of warm self-regard in which such an anger could
accumulate, form itself into a creature, a demon, to burst out
at me, in me, like that time in the peace and solemnity of the
Mass. That is why I will try to explain in what I am going to

write how it is that falsehood leads to tyranny and the impris-
onment of conscience. Only prayer and devotion will free us
from the torment and delusion of history. And yet the history
must needs be written, because the pain and chagrin of event is
compounded by the wilfulness and error of historians. My
work is to be – I have the title – *Foras Feasa ar Éirinn* – *The
Groundwork of Knowledge Concerning Ireland*.

I look around at the cabin: the pallet where I lie; my cloak, a
hempen shroud hung inside the door; the fire in the hearth
smoking beneath the pot where I boil my meat; the scrubbed
table; my books on a crude shelf made of discarded timbers
from an outhouse. This is where I've also hoped I would end,
oddly enough, ready to pray, ready to write. In blindness of
spirit, in despair at the thought of the labours ahead, I make
the first marks on the paper in the language I am proud to
inhabit. The language is that of Muircheartach Ó Condúin
and all his predecessors. It is Irish, not Latin or English: Irish.
It is what I live in. It is what I am. It is what will outlast me,
thanks be to God.

1921

TOM MULL

Tom Mull and his father were out on the Curragh Road on the southside of the city, making their collections of slop and leftovers for the pigs. The donkey would stand, head drooped, outside the little terraced houses as either father or son would go to the door with a galvanised bucket. 'Any waste for the pigs, mam?'

Then, if there were slops or vegetable peelings, or fatty ends of meat, they would be brought out and plopped into the bucket, already, in many cases, containing a heady swill. The bucket would then be brought out to the cart, squeaking on its metal handle, and the contents dumped into one of the three old milk churns that served as receptacles – one for fairly rotten waste; one for leavings that were relatively fresh; and the third for the bits and pieces that retained their springiness and bite. Together the churns gave off a strong smell in which none of the elements that had gone into its making could be discerned: there was instead a powerful uniform haze of rot, of food breaking down, digesting itself. It was not an unpleasant smell, Tom always thought: there was something reassuring about it, close, known.

Whenever there was a child in the house Tom's father would give it one of the little balloons he kept on the floor in the front of the cart. Each one was mounted on a little stick which also carried an array of pink and white and blue feathers. Tom would watch his father bend down to the child in the doorway, who would be standing in expectation, having been told there was something out in the cart. Patrick would lean forward and present the gift to the child with an air of solemn courtesy.

'These balloons,' he'd say, 'are special balloons from Shanghai, where special factories make them so that they bring a wish with them. But you've got to be a good child for the wish to come true.'

This night Tom watched his father turn away from the upturned face of a girl, left standing at the door, holding the feathered balloon, looking at it.

'Come on,' his da said. 'Time for home. It's past eight o'clock. The dinner will be ruined. And it's bacon ribs tonight.'

It was a Saturday in early summer. The air was still bright and lively, it having been a warm and sunny day. Tom never minded giving up his Saturdays like this for the collections out Turner's Cross and Evergreen Road. They always did well out this way. A good number of the people who lived in the small cottages worked as market gardeners on the large estates that extended over Ballyphehane out the Kinsale Road to the Black Ash and Togher, so they ate plenty of vegetables and were less scrupulous than those in other suburbs in the way they pared and cut them before cooking. There was more to be had out along here than in the big houses in Blackrock or St Luke's, for example.

They turned into the slightly uphill length of the Evergreen Road, which ran beneath a row of cottages looking down to the Convent of the Sacred Heart. The day had grown calm and still, and they looked up at the parapet of the convent, where the nuns walked in the clear golden light, black figures lit by radiance. They walked singly, passing each other without speaking, the cowled heads looking to the front, slightly down-cast all the time.

'There they are, boy, free of all the trouble of this life,' said Tom's father.

'But are they, though?' replied Tom.

They walked on in silence. The plaster rendering on the terraced houses on the Evergreen Road, and the red brick of the villas on Summerhill South gave off a sombre lustre in the evening light. They felt the donkey gratefully relax back into the harness as the decline towards Langford Row began. They passed the neat green gates of the Quaker Meeting House and burial ground. Would it not be calmer, thought Tom, to be one of those than to be in the Church to which he belonged? All rules and compulsions, and he'd heard that the Quakers had no rules, except honest dealing and telling the truth. But how could anyone tell the truth?

'Da,' he said, 'do you think you can tell the truth if you're not rich?'

'What do you mean?' said Patrick, taking his hand for a moment from the donkey's halter to squeeze her ears. She snorted, and got the scent of the water in the trough which lay, smooth and cool, at the bottom of Summerhill South.

'I just think that the poor are always looking for someone to help them, and that means they can never say anything to anyone who might go against them. The poor need people to think the best of them.'

'And the rich, I suppose you think,' said his da, 'can do what they like, say what they wish?'

'I suppose, yes, that's what I mean.'

'You'd better be careful with that kind of ruminating,' said old Mull. 'You'll give yourself headaches. Don't you know that the rich man never tells the truth except by accident? Anyway, that's what old Long used to say, God rest him, out in Carrignavar.'

'Why did he say that?'

'Because the rich man cannot tell the difference between what is true and what is not. And this ability, not to know the difference, he either acquires or inherits. And that's what the rich leave to their children.'

'What?'

'They leave to their children the ability to be indifferent.'

They came to the drinking trough and stopped. The donkey sank her jaws into the blue water and drew it in over her yellow teeth. In the brown doorway of the Railway Tavern stood Jim Condon looking out at the two Mulls. He'd come out of the bar to get a breath of summer evening air, and to clear his head a bit. He'd been at it since midday. His eyes hurt from the smoke of the bar and now smarted with the sudden brightness of the evening light. He called out: 'How are you, Mull. Plenty of scrap tonight for the pigs?'

'Good takings. Or leavings,' said Patrick, waving at him.

Jim turned back in. Poor man, he thought, soft in the head.

Tom and his father went on up Douglas Street and made for the artery of the city, the North and South Main streets.

'Late as it is,' said Patrick, 'we'll have a pint, Tom.'

They stopped outside the grey stone of the Old Weigh House, tied the donkey to an iron bollard, and went into the bar with its heavy semicircular counter. A group of three men stood at the counter: one, a thin balding man in a long grey coat brought the full pint to his mouth and, throwing back his head, the back of his neck contracting into four rolls of skin, he swallowed half the measure. He slowly replaced his glass on the counter, and watched the yellow film of froth descend the walls of glass to rejoin the creamy surface beneath. He breathed out. One of his companions, a tall stocky man with black hair, smiled broadly. 'Can't beat it, Dermot?'

The third was a brooding, querulous man, in a tweed suit and an unkempt red beard. 'How could anyone,' he said, obviously resuming a conversation, 'play a Beethoven concerto on a mouth organ?'

'I'm telling you,' the spindly bald man said, 'I saw it with my own two eyes in Cornmarket Street, in O'Neill's. He was, he said, from Zacopané in the Tatra Mountains in the south of Poland, and he'd been on the Seven Seas for twenty years, practising. Once I ever saw him. Then he was gone. Even though he said he'd come back the next night, but he didn't.'

Sitting alone, at a table beneath the window and obscured by the light from outside, was the other customer in the bar. With a shock Tom Mull saw, as he got used to looking against the still strong sunlight that was coming through the frosted glass, that the other man was his boss, Morgan Holmes. He had before him a half-drunk pint of stout and a glass of spirit of some kind, not whiskey. It was dark brown and Tom guessed it might be rum.

Holmes was stroking his chin in a calm and meditative way and looking straight ahead at a point in the panelling underneath the curved top of the bar. He wore a blue tweed suit and a plain crimson shirt with a blue tie. The jacket, hanging loose, revealed a gold fob chain looped to his waistcoat pocket. He moved his gaze, which travelled towards Tom and his father, resting it awhile on them, languidly nodding his pale face in recognition. He closed his eyes, and crossed and uncrossed his legs, placing one palm between his thighs. He motioned them over with the other in a slow gesture. The three drinkers at the bar fell silent at this show of recognition.

'Will you join me, Tom? And would your friend come over for a drink as well?' said Holmes.

Tom, unnerved by this, smiled and crossed over to where Holmes was sitting.

'Please, Mr Holmes, I'd like you to meet my father, Patrick Mull. Dad, this is Mr Holmes.'

Old Mull knew who the other man was. 'Pleased to meet you, sir. I knew your father, old Mr Holmes, God rest him.'

'Thank you. A drink?'

'I'll take a pint of stout, sir, and so will Tom, as long as you don't mind.'

'Why should I mind?'

'That an employee is drinking in a public bar.'

'And isn't the employer?'

'Well, that's different.'

'What's different? Isn't one man as good as another?'

'That may be so in theory, but in practice it often doesn't work out like that.'

'No. Thank goodness for that.'

The conversation subsided as the drinks were brought, Holmes getting another stout and ordering also a dark rum.

'I've been here,' said Holmes, 'since three o'clock. My wife sent me on an errand after lunch to buy water biscuits – which for some reason were overlooked in the weekly order from Woodford Bournes – and I'm afraid I allowed myself to be distracted. Not only that, I've not even got the biscuits.'

'And were you drinking on your own, sir?'

'Yes. The only way. Nothing interferes to disturb the concentration.'

Tom looked at his employer. The face was long and thin, one that does not easily lose its profile, but nevertheless there was a sagging in the jaw and a puffiness in the cheeks. The booze was well started on its work of destruction on the inside, but it interested Tom that someone's decline could have such clearly evident physical consequences. Why didn't he stop it? He had everything; Tom had nothing.

'It's a fine way to relax, the drink,' said Patrick Mull, 'but it's a terrible master.'

'It is that,' said Holmes, 'but maybe that's what some people want.'

'How?'

'Maybe some people, like me, for instance, need a hard master to make us happy. Only that way, maybe, can we be roused out of our laziness. I'm lazy, aren't I, Tom?'

'I don't think so, sir.'

It never entered Tom's mind to consider whether the man he worked for was lazy or not. It was irrelevant. He supposed that if he were Morgan Holmes, he'd be lazy. But it made no sense to think in these terms. Morgan Holmes was Morgan Holmes, and breathed a different kind of air. He was Tom Mull, and he breathed an atmosphere of pig swill and, in the mornings, that curious burnt toast smell that hung over the poor parts of Cork as he walked down Blarney Street towards the North Gate Bridge.

'Well,' continued Holmes, 'I think I'm lazy. There's never enough time to do what I want to do. Every day ends the same way, in bitterness and disappointment. Then the first slug of the bottle, which lifts the spirit. When I look at you, Tom, and your workmate, Michael Condon, I realise how much I miss the ordinary things of life.'

Patrick knew that there was something in the Holmes family history about illegitimacy, sex; a girl was involved, but it was all some time ago now. The lore of rumour in the town still retained some recollection of this scandal, but the same lore had it that the affair was hushed up. That the girl was no better than she should be. He decided to issue a probe. 'There's nothing like a clear conscience,' he said. 'Because once you have a clear conscience then you can go about your business in peace, and not be a trouble to yourself or others.'

'There are some minds, Mr Mull, that cannot experience that. There are some hearts that have hardened to such an extent that nothing can touch them. They awake to nothing.'

'No, sir, God is good.'

Tom looked at his father in surprise. His bald head glowed white in the light that now had begun to darken slightly in the bar. The three men at the counter had stopped all conversation, and were now listening in silence to this exchange. Underneath the smooth pate, Patrick's eyes had narrowed. The full lips were tightened. He was, Tom realised, like an animal closing on its prey. The mood of the conversation, however, still preserved an air of almost casual enquiry and comment.

'To you, maybe. Maybe to you God is good. To me. No. I don't think it's possible.'

'He never closes his door to us,' said Patrick.

'But he slams another,' said Holmes.

'You see, sir,' said Patrick, 'there is such a thing as the sin of pride, that will not or cannot remember God's mercy.'

'And there is such a thing,' said Holmes, 'as the impossibility of ever knowing that mercy, and knowing that some things will not be forgiven, not because God will not forgive, but because we can't forgive ourselves.'

'The sin of pride,' said Patrick.

'Or just admitting that you're damned?'

'The same thing,' replied Tom's father, his face now inclining into the shade.

'I don't know,' said Holmes, his eyes clouding with tears.

Oh my Jesus, thought Tom, he's going to cry. And indeed, yes, tears began to flow down Holmes's cheeks.

'I'm sorry,' he said. 'It's just that I can't get something out of my mind. Something that happened years ago.'

Holmes now began to be wracked with helpless sobs. His hand shook as he raised the rum to his lips. 'Oh hell,' he said.

Later that evening, as Tom and his father walked up Shandon Street, the older man turned to his son and stopped, just at the turn into Blarney Street. 'What did you think of that?'

'I feel sorry for him.'

'Don't.'

'Why?'

'He feels sorry enough for himself already. He's really a heartless bastard who cares about nothing but his own ease.'

Tom walked on beside his father, thinking how little he

knew about people.

When they walked in through the half-door they saw, in the fading light in the room before them, smoked bacon ribs on a large plate, a tureen of cabbage, a heap of potatoes, and a block of butter set in the middle of the scrubbed deal table.

1933

CON CONDON

I still like the quiet in here. There's no speech, just systems of hand gestures, movements of the head. It's so strange to be out of speech altogether. It is May and the hawthorns are in full flower; the ditches are thick with straggles of vetch in purple and white; the rock roses are starting to bud as well; and the foxgloves are opening up along their lengths. I'm still not used to noticing so much now that I don't speak any more. Even as I'm writing this, a thick yellow slant of light is slicing through my room. The wooden shutters are pulled back and the window is pushed open on its metal hinges. This slab of light contains a million moving specks of dust, agitated by the heat and presumably by my own breathing and physical presence. From outside, a trill of sound flows up out of the trees beneath: a thrush pouring out a lovely and complicated burst of singing that grows at first from a simple set of notes, then doubles back to shift them around until, after a pause, it returns again to break the re-formed pool of quiet, reawakening the flurry of notes and taking them through an extraordinary circuit of different sounds only to return once more back to the few simple notes and then the silence, full of waiting. Each time the bird utters these sounds it's like a shock. I offer a prayer; hoping that I may understand some day how all of this is related to the pain I feel when I think of the face of Christ dripping with blood.

I arrived here before Christmas, having taken the bus from Parnell Square. All I carried with me was a small Rexine holdall, which contained a flat razor and a leather sharpening strap, soap, a facecloth, and a change of underwear. The Prior had written to say that I could come with nothing if I wished. He was standing on the gravelled pathway between the arch of the entrance, his cowl pulled up against the driving rain.

'Happy Christmas, Con,' he said. 'You're very welcome here, and I hope you will be happy with all of the troubles of the world behind you.'

He put his arm around my shoulder and walked me in out of the rain, then turned back to greet the few other passengers who had got off: people who were going on retreat for a few days before the Christmas season. He brought us all into the refectory, which smelled of meat, potatoes, and polish, and sat us down at the end of a long scrubbed table. A brother, carrying a tray, came out from a door made of planed vertical boards. He set down mugs of black tea and plates with thick slices of buttered bread, nodded, then left.

'You know about our rule of silence,' said the Prior. 'Con here is joining us today, and as soon as he puts on his robe he'll also have to keep the silence.'

His words echoed around the large dining hall, and I

thought how strange a thing speech was. The Prior sat at the table, blessed himself, and said grace, stretching out his joined hands before him on the surface of the table. I watched the brown habit slide up his arms and looked at the locked hands strong and firm.

I was shown to my room, which the Prior called my 'cell', and given a brown robe smelling of lavender. I stripped off and put my suit, shirt, socks and shoes into a wooden box I'd also been given. I put on the robe, and the heavy rough cloth felt strange against my warm skin. I buckled on the pair of sandals, then sat down on the bed with its thin mattress, and prayed.

The Prior came back and took the box containing my clothes. 'You can have these back at any time. You know that. But welcome to the brotherhood of silence.' He smiled and pressed his index finger to his lips. 'Come.'

I walked with him along the gallery on to which my room opened, then went down the steps to the cloister, where two other monks were walking. A bell started to ring. All four of us walked together, us three allowing the Prior precedence. I watched the robes of the other brothers swaying with their stride. We passed an open space. It was still raining and we all lifted our cowls over our heads.

That first walk to the chapel is ingrained in my memory. I noticed everything: the angle of the rain, the feet of the monks in their worn sandals, the curved stone in the archways of the cloister, the slender pillars supporting the upstairs gallery, the red-berried holly tree in the centre of the close, the black earth of the empty flowerbeds, the yellow winter jasmine against a far wall, the heavy door to the chapel with the grain of the oak running against the cut of the wood, the dark interior, and the chanting of the monks in Latin.

I was, thank God, no longer Con Condon, but someone else. I knelt down and raised my eyes to the altar, white and luminous in the dark. Incense burned in the thurible, which a brother swung on its hissing chains. A priest took the spiked monstrance, the host at its centre, and with a sudden and

triumphal gesture, lifted it over his head, and held it there. All
heads bowed.

I miss my garden at Mr Sless's, and the privacy and comfort
of my cabin. I went to work for Jacob Sless after I left the job
on the cousin's farm out in Rathcooney. His garden, and his
brother Cecil's across the road, were my responsibility, but
together they came to no more than three acres in all. I kept
the driveways clear of weeds, pruned the rhododendrons, kept
the vegetable gardens, and planted out the beds for cut flowers.
I hanked the onions and hung them from the joists in the shed,
stored the potatoes in a specially dug pit, lined and covered
with sand, and made a herb garden out of a waste bit of ground
to the side of the house. The herb garden gave Mr Sless particular pleasure. A few weeks after I'd started, when the heap of
nettles and broken stones and bits of glass had started to annoy
me, I began to clear it up. I kept the stones but took out all the
glass and pieces of rusty iron. Once the rubbish was cleared
away I realised that the earth was quite good in this sunny
corner, but I mixed sand into it, then a few barrows of
compost from the heap, along with some farmyard manure
I'd had sent in from Rathcooney. I made a circular bed, with
a pathway through it constructed from the stones I'd salvaged,
so that as well as giving access to the bed, now quite large, they
made a kind of rockery as it were, giving necessary shade for
certain plants. In February I planted into the now sweetened
earth thyme, hyssop, rosemary, mint, sage, parsley, borage,
and a long angelica. Everything took almost immediately. By
June the same year I could walk out of my cabin in the
evening, cup of tea in hand, and smell the savours rising from
the herb garden. More often than not Mr Sless would be
standing in the French windows, wearing his silk smoking
jacket, looking out at me and smiling.

I decided to leave one evening when Mr Sless had invited me
in to join himself and his brother Cecil for what they called one
of their 'chats'. I'd cut the privet hedge that day. It was towards
the end of summer, and as I walked up the brick path from my

cabin to the house I got the smell of the privet flowers from the
pile of cuttings I'd left to burn when they'd dried out a bit. I
looked up at the red-tiled roof, with its elaborate ridge of
carved cast iron, and thought how restful it all was.

Jacob Sless and his brother were in the library, sitting on
each side of a green baize table, the chessboard before them.

'Come in, Con,' said Jacob, 'sit down and be our adjudi-
cator. Drink? Help yourself.'

I poured, as I always did, a small sherry from the decanter on
the grand piano. The brothers also had their tiny little glasses of
dark blue plum brandy at the side of the chessboard. I watched
Cecil move his knight and looked at Jacob's impressive face.

Cecil spoke. 'You must tell us, Con, what your plans are. Do
you wish to marry? We, my brother and I, would like to plan
so that you're well prepared for such an eventuality. There are
nice little houses being built at the top of High Street, a new
park called Marble Arch. It's near the railway line, but the
houses, semidetached villas, are very pretty and well built. I
stopped by today and checked the quality of the timber in the
windows and it's excellent: good seasoned pine, with the resin
still smelling fresh. I think, Con, we'd like to buy one for you
and come to an understanding. We could allow you a mortgage privately, and deduct the payments from you weekly.
You'd eventually, after perhaps ten years, own your house.'

'You see,' said Jacob, 'we appreciate you, Con. You are
honest and hardworking, and they are rare qualities. Very rare.
And we have to ensure that you're happy, and that, through a
little planning, you'll be comfortable and secure in life as you
get older. It's this planning that I think we should undertake
now.'

I didn't fully understand what these two men were offering,
but I knew it was an act of pure kindness.

'I think, Mr Sless, sir, and you, too, sir' – to Cecil – 'that you
are both gentlemen, true gentlemen who are concerned for
other people. But you see, and I hope you don't mind me
saying this, I'm not sure that I ever want to marry. It doesn't

seem to enter my head.'

The brothers looked at each other. Jacob smiled. 'You're lucky,' he said. 'Most young men think of nothing else but girls. You are unusual in your contentment.'

'I'm not bothered by them, sir,' I said. 'I know what you mean, but out in Rathcooney, when some of the lads would be lingering behind on the way home from the crossroads, waiting for the girls to catch up, I'd never be that interested. While they would be frisky as ponies, jumping up and down on the ditch, kicking gates, swinging off branches of trees. Maybe there's something wrong with me, but all of this excitement of the nerves never troubles me.'

'That's as may be,' said Cecil, 'but don't worry. The time will come probably when you'll change your mind. You can't escape nature, unless you are one of the very few exceptions.'

The houses of Jacob Sless and his brother were places of deep quiet. Their wives, one from a law family in Cork, the other of merchant stock in Dublin, moved about the houses with a serene and confident slowness. The kitchen towels were neatly folded on shelves in the cool darkness of their pantries, beside the rows of condiments and chutneys prepared from surplus garden produce: from marrows, tomatoes, apples, pears, and quinces. Their sitting rooms, where the women and daughters wrote their letters or made their diary entries, smelled persistently of lavender, disposed in drawers and davenports in linen sachets. The sombre restraint of this family life I did not find reassuring at all, though it was a great contrast to the turbulence I was used to at home. With Ma and Da and all the others there were always clashes of anger or temperament; but out here on the Douglas Road, the politeness and silence made me nervous, where at home I was abashed. How could those women in the Sless housholds sit so still for so long? I wondered. What do they do when they're finished their diaries? How can they spend so much time reading? Whenever I'd spend half an hour in the kitchen, drinking a glass of milk, or having a light meal maybe, one of the women would open up bits and pieces of conversation, but I always thought they went nowhere. I felt saddened, somehow, when I left the kitchen and their presence. I liked the perfume of cologne from them; they always smelt clean and fresh, a rebuke almost to my own toilsome odours, but I was invariably pleased to be walking down the pathway to the potato drills or the onion beds.

Was I an exception? Not drawn by the instinct to make a home with someone? I liked the solitude of my cabin: the bare planked walls, the narrow strips of flooring, the wooden single bed, the black stove for heating and cooking, fuelled by turf and sawn blocks. I kept my books on a small table with uneven legs, so it rocked when I laid my elbows on it, as I often did when I closed my eyes to concentrate, putting the base of my palms against the shape of my eyeballs behind their lids. My books were those I have now: the Bible, the *Imitation of Christ*, and a few others.

'I think, sir,' I replied to Mr Sless's statement about nature tending to insist that we follow its dictates, 'that I may be an exception.'

Again the brothers exchanged glances, and Jacob moved his queen in a long diagonal right into the heart of Cecil's defensive position before the back line.

'In what way?'

'I think I may have a vocation to the monastic life.'

'Oh,' said Jacob.

Cecil looked at me, and nodded.

'If that is so,' said Jacob, 'we wish you well and remember to pray for us.'

I do this for those two gentlemen every day of my life. The bell rings, and I imagine the walk before me, down along the gallery, the sun warm on my shoulders, the smells rising from the warmed earth, and the lemony perfume from the tiny white flowerets hidden under the glossy leaves of the big holly tree.

1903

MARY O'DWYER

It wasn't long after we came to Leeds that the trouble began. I didn't know what I was thinking of to leave Cork the way I did, in the condition I was in, but that experience of being hounded by old Holmes, with his crafty eyes taking everything in and saying nothing, trying to get me terrified so I'd give way to him, left me completely confused. So that when Jim made that offer I was so shocked by his kindness, especially after the blow I'd had from Holmes in his freezing office, that I just caved in. And I never regretted it, not really. It was a manly thing for him to do, and I think that manliness must always be unexpected and generous. As we know, we're all of us only too used to the expected and the mean-hearted. So I

agreed with Jim's plan.

We talked it over the next day, me lying in a man's bed for the first time in my life, watching him, his braces holding up his trousers crossing on his bare back, as he made me tea and toast. The first time ever a man prepared food for me. He was in his bare feet, and as he turned towards me, I saw his flat stomach above his baggy trousers and my heart lifted. Holding the tray in one hand, like a waiter in the Victoria, he did a little dance, swiftly crossing his elegant feet in a kind of two-step. We laughed out loud, but then he put his finger to his lips and pointed down. 'The Academy Dairy will be wondering what's going on,' he said.

We ate the food, toast thickly cut and dripping with salted butter, and I drank the strong sweetened tea in huge gulps.

'Are you still game?' he said.

I told him I was. And I told him that the man who had betrayed me was someone whose father he had driven around the city on many occasions. For the first time I spoke his name to someone else. Morgan Holmes. Jim said nothing. I got out of bed and dressed slowly, giving him plenty of time to watch me as he lay back on the bed. I then went to Elliott Holmes's office and was allowed in immediately as soon as he was told who it was. I said I would go to Leeds, but that I wanted enough money to keep me going. I told him I wouldn't settle for less than fifty pounds.

He tried to get out of this, saying that it would be dangerous for me to carry that amount of money around with me; that he'd send it to the convent he'd book me into; and that the sisters would keep it safe for me. Ten pounds would be enough to be going on with. I said, no, that I'd look after it myself, and I repeated that I would not settle for anything else. I did not say, of course, that I had an escort, and that I'd absolutely no intention of going to the Convent of the Adorici, as he called it, or of having anything to do with whatever branch of holy nuns he'd come in contact with through whatever underhand means a Cork Protestant uses to deal with a Catholic girl his son's got into trouble.

'I think, sir,' I said, wondering where I was getting all this cheek from, 'I think you'd better pay up.'

He stared at me from under those eyebrows of his that look like thatch hanging over the door of a house, and produced his wallet. He counted out the notes: forty-five pounds.

'No,' I said, 'fifty.'

Jim and I then packed a few bags – he had little, I had less – and we hired a pony and trap down to Camden Quay to take ship for Fishguard. I went into the offices of the Cork Steam Packet Company and with Jim's help I sent a telegram to my mother, letting her know that all was well and not to worry. From Fishguard we took a train to Leeds, where we arrived that night, and stayed in the Queen's Hotel near the station in Wellington Street.

It was late when we arrived, but we booked in, Jim brazenly putting us down as Mr and Mrs Condon, taking no notice of the pointed way that the desk clerk looked at the ringless wedding finger of my left hand. The lift was operated by this young fellow in a pillbox hat with a strap around his chin, wearing a blue uniform with red stripes down the legs.

'Can we get anything to eat?' Jim asked the lift boy.

'It's late, sir, the kitchens are closed,' replied the lad, in an accent so thick and strange it nearly made me laugh.

'Look, this might help,' said Jim, giving the boy a pound note, and throwing him a gamey wink. 'And,' he says, 'bring us something from the bar', giving him another two shillings.

'Certainly, sir. Anything else?'

'Not a bit of it. We've got all we need.'

We all three of us then collapsed laughing. I had to lean against the mirror in the lift and the boy hung his head as his shoulders shook, while Jim was bending over holding his stomach. There were tears in my eyes. I hadn't laughed so much in years.

We got to the room and the boy showed us in. It was

painted pink, with a powder-blue carpet. There was a massive bed, and above it a huge chandelier. I went to the window and looked out over Queen's Square. It was eleven o'clock and the streets were still busy. Trams pulled up and drew away from the big building opposite, and from below our window there was the racket of steel crashing on steel, the voices of people shouting their goodnights, and a few late flower-sellers trying to get rid of their remaining blooms.

'Go down,' said Jim to the boy, 'like a good fellow and bring us up the drinks, and would you also get a bunch of flowers for the lady here. That's no lady,' he added, 'that's my . . .'

This was enough to send us all into fits again, but the boy went off, and Jim came up to me, pushed me on to the bed, and kissed me long and hard.

'You're a great girl,' he said, as he stroked my hip beneath my long, tight-fitting dress.

'I'm not,' I said. 'You know I'm not.'

'I didn't say good, did I? I said great. Horse of a different colour. Giddy-up.'

The boy came back with a huge spray of carnations and marigolds, and little flowers with the most delicate perfume I'd ever smelt. I asked the boy what they were as I put them into the vase he'd also brought up on a trolley along with the drinks.

'They're called freesias,' he said. 'They're supposed to come from Switzerland.'

I inhaled the soft odour again and I thought of mountains and streams, and the darkness slowly falling.

Jim took up a green bottle from a silver bucket, and poured out yellow champagne into long glasses for the three of us.

'Here's to you both,' said the boy. 'May you have much happiness and success here in Leeds. I propose a true Yorkshire toast: to the Irish and to Yorkshire.'

'To Yorkshire,' said Jim, swallowing his drink in one large gulp.

'Here,' said the boy, 'that's not Guinness, you know.'

'No,' said Jim. 'What else have you got?'

We drank whisky, wine, a pitcher of dark beer the lad brought up from the bar, and we ate like horses: cold roast beef, cold boiled potatoes with a salad dressing on them, beet-root in a sweet sauce, pickled onions and small cucumbers (called 'gherkins', we were told), pork pies with thick crusts packed with spicy meat and amber, clarified jelly, and thick pastries larded with cream and strawberry jam. The boy shared the lot with us, and kept going down to the bar for yet more wine and champagne. The last bottle he brought up, he stood in the door with it and lifted it up before him. It was an ancient, dusty old bottle, still cob-webbed, the label peeling off. He held the long cork in his other hand. 'I drew it in the lift on the way up,' he said. 'The longest I've ever seen.' He poured the wine into three glasses. The colour was so dark it was almost black.

Jim tasted. 'It's like drinking the night,' he said. 'Here's to the night.'

'To the night,' we said, echoing him.

It was a Châteauneuf-du-Pape, 1847. I remember the label, and the heavy weight of the bottle when I lifted it the following morning.

We found a flat in Headingley, on the Shire Oak Road, the next day. Jim had some contacts out on the York Road. He got a job working with a builder out there, with the promise of something better soon, seeing as he was a skilled man and a qualified driver.

It was no more than a week before the trouble began. But no matter what, I'll never forget Jim's kindness, and that night of feasting will always be with me, to think of in the privacy of my own thoughts, not caring if the whole thing was a sin or not. It's little enough sinning that's ever been done by the likes of me. And a bit of it never harmed anyone. Jim taught me the joy of sin; Holmes only taught me its pain.

1847

PATSY CONDON

He woke in the early morning, before the dark had thinned. The small window was a pale square of grey light. He could make out the features of the child lying beside him in the narrow bed. She was asleep, her face still. Her thin arm was clasped about his neck, and he could smell the breath coming from her open mouth. It was sweet and wholesome. The teeth were firm and white, and the gums pink and healthy. He moved his face close to her hair and inhaled its odour, a mixture of warm hay and mountain heather. They'd arrived in Queenstown the previous night and found these lodgings in a back street above a public house. They shared the room with a husband and wife come in all the way from Caherciveen, also headed for America. They were quiet people, who sat in silence, but shared their bread with them last night, and their few strips of cooked bacon. Then they had all prayed for protection on the journey.

The child awoke. He could see from her eyes that for a moment there was a surge of panic in her. She didn't know where she was or who he was.

'It's all right, Maureen. I'm here. You're in Queenstown. And today's the day we start our big adventure.'

He was terrified at the thought of the boat, the huge holds crammed with people, the crushing and pushing getting on. His stomach was sick with fear, and he realised he was holding it tense and taut. He relaxed it. He thought of his fiddle and the music he could make with it, the satisfaction of the long notes held deep in a slow air as the people listening sighed their satisfied grief.

'Let's get ourselves ready, Maureen, and we'll see if there's something to be had for breakfast.'

They got up and took their few belongings, Patsy carefully positioning his bundle so it did not swing against the wall as he went down the narrow wooden stairs. They paid and left.

Outside, they got the smell of fresh bread. At the corner stood an old man, before him a sheet of blackened metal under which burned a bed of turf sods, fanned to redness by the morning breeze. Flat cakes of bread were baking on the metal. To one side there were also a few kippers curling up in the heat. They bought bread and a piece of fish, and they ate it sitting down on a large corner stone set into the wall of a house nearby.

It was early but already large numbers of people were moving down towards the docks. Patsy and the girl joined them. He looked at their thin white faces, the stooped shoulders of the women, and the confident swagger of some of the men, top coats blowing open, hats tilted back, swinging their blackthorns as they called jocosely to each other.

'No harm to leave this godforsaken place.'

'There'll be fine times ahead.'

'Give us a swig of the bottle.'

'Sing a song.'

Other men, some so exhausted from walking they could scarcely shuffle, kept their heads down, or held the hand of a daughter or son. The children were mostly impassive, carrying large bags of provisions or utensils, some with pots strung around their shoulders, which clanked as they walked. One or two held tight to a little rag doll, or a knitted toy – a lamb or dog, soiled with continual hugging. The streets were crammed with people, all moving, and when they got to the quayside there were thousands there before them, twenty or so deep at the dock, all pushing forward and jostling. Every now and then, as Patsy could see from the slight height he stood on before going down into the throng, someone would be pushed off the quay wall into the water. This would be met with howls of derision and mockery, as the person below tried to swim fully clothed and burdened with luggage to the nearest set of steps. If he or she couldn't swim or if a child had been pushed over, a looped rope would be flung down, or eventually someone would jump in and help them out. Even so, Patsy could see there would be drownings unless the crowd thinned out. There were four or five boats at the dockside, sails furled, with sailors busily slopping water across the decks and others scrubbing the timbers with large wooden brushes held in both hands. Other men sat up on the rigging, mending sails, or greasing pulleys from large canisters of fat.

Patsy noticed that further up the quayside, beyond a small inlet, where a stream met the sea, stood another ship, away from the rest, with only a straggle of people on the dock beside it. He decided to make his way up to the boat, which he could only do by going back through the streets again as there was no way across to the upper dock from the one he looked down upon. He started back, even though Maureen said she didn't want to walk any more.

'I'll carry you,' he said.

He stooped down, and pulling his bundle round to his front, allowed her to climb onto his back.

'Hold on tight,' he said.

He felt her small arms around his shoulders tighten as he stood up again. She was so light. He walked into the oncoming crowd who looked at him in puzzlement, some asking where he was going.

'I'm just going back. It's too crowded,' he said. To which some would reply that it was always this way. Every day the quays were full. People stayed there night and day until they found a ship. There were no queues, just every man for himself. 'No, I'll take my chance,' he said.

When he got away from the docks the streets were quieter. He took a diagonal direction over towards where he thought the stream might be that he had to cross. He came down a narrow dirty street, which smelled of human excrement and cabbage, and there beneath him was the stream with five smooth stepping stones across it. Each stone had a name carved on its side, and the surface was worn to a glassy silkiness by many feet. A woman sat by a house on the other side. She wore a black cloak pulled up over her head, wisps of grey hair stirring slightly in the faint breeze. She was opening clams with a knife, taking them from a pot, then putting them into a basket. When she lifted them out from the black pot they had tendrils of green hanging from them. She looked up at him as he came towards her from the stream, her eyes set in a mass of soft wrinkles.

'You'll be hungry, I'm sure,' she said to him, looking at the child on his back. 'Everyone has hunger on them these days.'

'No thank you,' said Patsy, looking at the shellfish, and getting their rich wholesome smell.

'Take one or two,' she said, 'if only for the little one. I cooked them with nettles, so they'll clean the blood. The best thing for a sea journey, to have clean blood.'

He stopped and looked down into the clams in their mess of

nettles. She opened four and gave them to him, two of which he ate on the spot, tilting the shell back, she having dislodged the meat inside, so the sea-tasting morsels went down his throat in one swallow. He gave two to the child, who had clambered to the ground, and she did likewise, even though at first she wrinkled up her nose when she looked at the big black shells.

'May God be with you,' said the old woman, 'and remember always to give to the poor. Because you will be a wealthy man once the misfortunes are past. They will pass. You have taken a fortunate step to come this way. You're headed for the small boat on the far quay?'

'Yes, we are.'

'It's the best of the lot of them. My own husband is the master of it. He's never been able to get a mooring on the main dock, but although this used to put him out for a long time, because he wouldn't take the soup like all the other mariners have to do in order to get a mooring there, it now doesn't matter to him. He sees what goes on at the main dock every day: bribery, prostitution, anything at all to get a passage. But my man will only take what's comfortable and safe. The other boats are no better than they're called: 'coffin ships'. Tell my husband you spoke to his wife when you get to his ship. He's called Captain Tracy, and my name is Elizabeth, Elizabeth Tracy. God be with you, young man, and your daughter.'

Maureen was tickling a kitten that had tumbled out of the dark hallway of the house and was now rolling on its back pretending to fight with the child's hand. Patsy was going to explain that she was not his daughter, but decided not to. What else was she now but his own?

'I am deeply beholden to you,' he said to the old woman.

'Remember what I said. Remember what was said to you in the Cobh of Cork this day by Elizabeth Tracy, whose husband will see you safely over the waves to America.'

Patsy stooped and allowed Maureen to climb up again. They went through the straggly streets, walking over a light mast of sand and crushed shells until they came to the upper dock. On the quay below Patsy saw the milling crowds, the people shouting and howling, every now and then someone going over into the filthy water. A gangway was let down from one of the boats and people were ascending it in single file, but at the quayside there was a large bunch of men and women, flailing wildly at each other as they strove to get near the end of the roped walkway, money clenched in their hands, proffering it to the three sailors who controlled access to the vessel.

At the quayside on which Patsy stood there were no more than twenty or thirty people, sitting around and talking. Leaning over the side of the ship, his elbows on the gunwale, smoking a long clay pipe, was the man Patsy took to be Captain Tracy. He waved up at him.

The man smiled and waved back. 'Do you want passage?' he shouted.

'Yes, for me and the girl. I am told to say that I met Elizabeth Tracy.'

'Well, I'm sorry for your troubles,' said the man, 'but you've survived the experience. You're welcome. Would the little girl like to come aboard and see the ship?'

'I'd like that,' said Maureen, over Patsy's head. The two men laughed.

The man and the girl climbed the shaking gangplank, Maureen before Patsy, holding on to the rope as she carefully put her bare feet on the separate timbers that made up the walkway. He noticed her slender feet and tiny ankles black from the road.

1952

MICHAEL CONDON

It was, I remember, one of those mornings – and there were a lot of them round that time – that I woke up feeling utterly tired out. I'd had one of those nights when I kept on waking up, but in the morning as I broke out of sleep I could recall almost nothing of what I had dreamt, just a confused feeling of unhappiness. I've always put this feeling – and I often get it in the mornings, first thing – down to something in my character, a touch of morbidity maybe, or just a jangle of the nerves. But I've noticed, too, that whenever it gets very bad – and by bad, I mean a tension so fierce you can hardly move in the bed without pain – I've noticed that it's a sign that something nasty is in the wind. Young Christopher came into the room. He poked his head round the door first and smiled and asked could he come in. So I told him he could and then Teresa woke up, too, and he climbed into the bed and snuggled up between the two of us, still smelling soapy from his bath the night before.

In spite of the ache of the tension, especially in my thighs, and in spite of the dry discomfort in my eyes, I reached out to him where he lay, turned to his mother, and put my hand through his thick dark hair. He put his hand up and caught mine and asked me to stop, saying that I was tickling him. When he laughed he wheezed slightly, a sound that made me shrink up with fear inside in a wave of shock as I realised how fragile his life was. He was a delicate child, too frail probably; and these thoughts went through me as I looked at the two slender bones at the back of his neck as he arched up to kiss his mother. But I thought then that I should put these thoughts out of my mind: the priest in St Augustine's had told me the Saturday before in confession that these morbid thoughts were just the actions of the devil, trying to deprive us of the consolations of faith. Put your trust in Jesus and His Blessed Mother, he said. They will watch over you and guard you from these promptings of despair. But it seemed that these feelings had a life of their own and could creep in under any protection I could ask for from on high.

I knew that I seemed to spend most of my time thinking about death and dying, and it seemed to hang over the house, almost like an invisible fog of some kind. In the church, praying, or just looking at the yellow lights of the candles, death seemed to back away somewhat, but outside of the church I'd never know when the fear would invade me, like some kind of acid in my bones, making every nerve in my body electric with worry. I could never talk to anyone about all of this, either, apart from the priest in the confession box. And it's not that I didn't try; because I'd visit Katherine, say, while Tim my brother-in-law would be on the four-to-twelve shift, and I'd attempt to get across to her something of what I was feeling and suffering, but I couldn't. I'd end up complaining about someone, or the government, or the clergy, or the city hall. And I'd see her getting fed up listening to me, and she'd say something like – Why don't you go into politics with all these ideas of yours? I was depressed, I suppose, but I couldn't think of any reason why.

And then, this day, the fear came out of its hiding place in the heart or in the instincts. We got up out of the bed, and I gathered young Christopher out of the bedclothes, keeping a blanket around him, and carried him into his own little room, and dressed him. His body was as smooth as milk and white and warm. I looked at his thin chest, and the ribs visible through the skin, the print of his collar bone under his delicate, sharply defined, Condon chin. The same chin that everyone in the family has, slightly jutting forward from the jawbone, which goes back in a straight line to turn up at a sharp angle to the ear. When I'd dressed him I held him close to me and felt his arms around my shoulders, hugging me with their slight but heartbreaking force.

I stood up and told him to come on into the kitchen, that I'd cook him his porridge for his breakfast, and that I'd give him the cream off the milk. I brought in the brown jug with the fat belly – when I called it that it always made him laugh – and poured off the thick warm cream from the top onto his porridge. I sugared it then, putting plenty on, digging into the blue bag on the dresser with a large spoon. When Teresa came in he was eating away and banging his feet against the bar of the chair beneath the seat. I finished my own breakfast and said goodbye to the two of them there in the dark kitchen, shadowed by my own premonitions.

I wish I didn't have these things but they seem to be in the family, an ability to smell disaster coming. I've seen Ma use this to avoid trouble or avert it, but I don't seem to have enough coldness in me to gain sufficient distance from these feelings to be able to take the necessary evasive action. I'm always in the thick of things, mixing premonition with fear, and anxiety with dread.

On the drive into town I took the usual route, past the Lough Chapel, down the Lough Road, down the Bandon Road, then Barrack Street, and over the bridge to Holmes's wholesale stores. I was early, as always, and I parked the car at the side of the brick wall, next to Mr Holmes's space where he parked his Triumph Mayflower. I unlocked the gate and pushed it back along the metal rails, going into the office where Tom Mull and I would sit thirty years or more before, when I started out at Holmes's, my lunch strapped to the carrier tray of my bicycle. Tom had now been in the States for many years, and, from what I'd heard, was doing well. Everyone seemed to do well out there. I went into the office and sat down to look at the order book for the day. The light was dull and grey and I switched on an anglepoise lamp over the desk.

I heard Mr Holmes's car pull up outside, the door slam, and in he walked. Looking the worse for wear as usual. He was drinking so heavily now that you couldn't tell from one minute to the next what mood he'd be in. Although his behaviour had been erratic for a long time, over these last few years it would be nothing for him, in one morning, to shout and scream at me over a trivial matter, then laugh uproariously at the insulting behaviour of a customer, then apologise to me, tears in his eyes, for speaking to me in the way he had. I tried not to take too much notice, saying to myself that we all had our troubles, and Tom had always said that Holmes had a guilty conscience over something he had done or left undone in his past.

Now he walked in with the careful walk of the hungover drunk. He came up to me in what I regarded now as 'my' office, and leaned over the desk, hands on the timber, fingers splayed. He then said to me something I'll never forget – that he never wanted to see me again in his place and that he'd had enough of my wasteful ways. He started to shout then, saying I was a bastard, over and over. I asked him please to stop, told him he didn't know what he was saying. He was shaking with rage, and told me to get out of his sight. He told me that I was a drab's melt, a whore's leavings, a fishwife's cunt. His voice had started to crack. I told him to calm himself down. Did he want something from down the road, from Galvin's? No, he didn't. He wanted rid of me and my miserable face for ever. That if he could get away with it, he'd drown me in the river outside the door. That he'd like to lock me into a chicken coop and keep me there until I'd die in my own shit. I wanted to know why he hated me and he said he'd sooner cut my throat than explain himself to me or to that walking pox, my mother.

It dawned on me. It *dawned* on me. At last, after all these years. The looks, the laughing, the mockery, Holmes's own disregard and insults. I was his *son*. I said this and he caught the lamp in his right hand and smashed it down into my neck. I then stood up. I didn't know what to say to him, except that this was no way for a father to treat a son. I couldn't think of anything else to say. Nothing else. All I could think of was my own little boy out in Togher and I hoped he'd never have to go through what I was going through that minute. In that minute I died. No doubt about it. I am a dead man.

1864

PATSY CONDON

He stood in the darkened bar, staring at himself in the mirror behind the racked bottles of spirits and wines. He was drinking a light beer from a long fluted glass, which gleamed in the yellow light from the gas filaments hissing on the walls. The place was quiet.

Fergal O'Dowd came in, a tall man, with short-cropped red hair. He strode over to Patsy Condon and stood before him, appraising him silently for a moment before speaking.

'Mr Condon, I understand you're from north Cork.'

'Yes, north Cork, Tipperary border.'

'I'm from Clonakilty myself, the other side of the county.'

'So I hear.'

'What can I do for you? They tell me you're a member of the Emmet Association over here.'

'Yes, I joined a couple of years ago while I was in the Bowery, but I have to say that I haven't been doing very much.'

'Well, we all have our different responsibilities.'

'That's why I wanted to speak with you. I hope I can talk in confidence.'

'Certainly,' said O'Dowd.

There was no sign of commitment or even interest from him. Patsy knew his reputation as a swift decisive organiser, as a man to be trusted. He was reassured by the remoteness he felt in the man, an icy readiness, a collected awareness. He'd served his time.

'Would you like a drink before I tell you the reason why I've asked to meet you?'

'Whiskey, please.'

The bald barman, called over, fussily poured a whiskey for O'Dowd, leaving the bottle on the counter, and, pulling up the suspenders on his shirt, drew off another beer for Patsy. The men waited until the barman had withdrawn to a corner of the bar, where, under a red lampshade, he was reading a dime novel about Billy the Kid. They heard the page turning in the silence. Patsy spoke, in Irish.

'Do you mind if we use Irish?'

'Not at all. Carry on.'

'It's a terrible thing that I have to tell you, and I must beg you to keep it to yourself, buried in your heart. You can help me, maybe, but if you can't and I wouldn't blame you if you refuse, then I want you to lock what I have said in your chest and to throw away the key.'

'You can rely on my silence,' said O'Dowd, nodding.

Patsy felt in himself a flood of gratitude at the sense of being completely understood. 'In speaking at all to you about what I have to say I am putting myself in danger, but I do not have any other choice.'

'Carry on.'

'It concerns my daughter, my adopted daughter, Maureen, whom I took with me from Queenstown on an emigrant ship after she'd been abandoned by her family in '47. I can't be exactly sure about her age, but she would be about twenty-one or twenty-two. I've reared her myself, and we've done reasonably well out here. I have a small music shop, and she has her own little business, too, a flower kiosk near the tram terminal in the Bronx. She's taken up with this fellow, an Italian who kept on coming into the kiosk and pestering her until she went out with him. Now he's starting to abuse her.'

'How?'

'He beats her up. She tries to pretend that they are accidents but she knows very well that I know the reason. All joy has gone out of her. She's lost in sadness.'

'Why don't you put a stop to it? Why are you talking to me about it?' asked O'Dowd.

'She loves him, I think, but I don't want to see her suffer. She's suffered enough as it is. I can't do anything. If I touch him, the Italian gang will see to me, or to her. He must be controlled, but his own crowd must do it, not me, or you, or anyone else other than the Italians themselves. That is why I'm talking to you. You can speak to them, to tell whoever it is that counts that a girl is being badly treated. I am sure they will listen to you.'

'I see.'

'I promise, if you help, I'll do anything you want me to do. I'm sure there are many tasks that need attention, or if I can help with money, I'll give whatever is within my means.'

'No one is ever asked to do what lies beyond them,' replied O'Dowd. 'Drink up. Let's go. I'd like to meet your daughter first.'

They went out into the sunshine of a New York late after-noon. On the dirt roadway tram cars jangled past, a delivery dray, pulled by a large brown shire horse, stopped outside a Hungarian delicatessen, while the black driver lifted from big wire-meshed meatsafes heavy smoked hams and red salami. The window of the shop was steamed up by the hot bread stacked in rows, and to one side a soup urn simmered, its sharp aroma drifting out on to the street. Patsy was amazed, as he always was, at the sheer quantity of food this city prepared and consumed for itself each day.

They took a tram to the Manhatten Transfer, near where Patsy's daughter had her kiosk. It was a small octagonal construction made of cast iron, with a serving hatch surrounded by blossoms. Inside there was room for no more than two or three people. Patsy introduced O'Dowd as a friend from Ireland. He was surprised to see how O'Dowd became animated and outgoing in the conversation with Maureen.

'What's your favourite flower, Maureen?' he asked.

'Jasmine, from the southern states, but it doesn't last very long. The smell is beautiful,' she replied.

O'Dowd noticed the yellow bruise on her upper jaw, an angry stripe running along her cheekbone and beneath her eye. 'You've had an accident?'

Maureen blushed, and O'Dowd took in her dark hair, fine white skin, and darting brown eyes. Her upper body tapered in what were almost two straight diagonals from her armpits to her waist. She moved quickly and briskly, snatching up a few roses, and re-arranging them in a vase already filled with flowers to hide her embarrassment. A customer appeared at the counter, and she turned to serve him in a deft, sweeping bustle of movement.

When she'd finished O'Dowd said again: 'You've had an accident.'

Maureen looked at her father, then lowered her eyes and said, yes, she had, but made no attempt to explain it away.

Later, back in the bar, O'Dowd spoke to Patsy in Irish, asking what he wanted done.

'I want him stopped.'

'But how much damage do you want done to him. If she likes him, there's a difficulty.'

'If she loves him, then it's all the more important that he be taught manners,' said Patsy.

'I'll speak to someone and enough will be done to ensure that what courtesy he doesn't have from nature he'll be taught by man.'

'I'm satisfied. I don't want to come between them, because that would only make matters worse. What must I do in return for them, the Italians?'

'You won't have to do anything for them. But you may be called to do something for us.'

'You know I'll do it,' said Patsy.

He called the barman from where he sat under the red lamp, still reading his book, and asked for two large ones. The job was done. Patsy's stomach soured as the whiskey went down.

1602

MOUNTJOY

The crawling fever. The ague. The cramp. The distress of the spirit. Victory is shallow. It is now a mere fact. No longer something in the blood or in the heart or in the mind. A fact. An accomplishment, perhaps. It will not improve anything. Before going into an engagement, on the march to it, the night before in the camp, the men bragging and drinking, it seems as if at last life is to be put to a reckoning. The night with no sleep. The reality of fear as the morning dawns. What is it to be afraid? To be an expert in the witnessing of every movement of the body, every stir of circumstance. To be so alert that the mind is pained with awareness. The seeing of everything.

The avoidance of any sense that there is an *I* or a *you*: only the differing flow of things happening. There is an understanding that events do not unfold; there are, it becomes apparent, monstrous gulfs of dark between the lifting of a hand and the grasping of the halter. Watching a man place his foot in a stirrup then lift his body heavy with armour onto the body of the horse, right leg sailing out over the animal's back, is watching a complicated and unnerving set of actual negotiations full of unforeseen dimensions. Cataclysm. An omnivalent set of motions each of which has its own possible ramifications; taken together the mysteriousness of action unmans the mind. This is fear. Every true soldier must know it to its uttermost, so that all impulse becomes fraught with danger, which leads to anger, which leads to what is required: the impetus towards the outcome, never caring what it may be. It is the rush that counts. The surge, the impetuous forward-thrusting drive. Blount. Blunt.

But, being over, the surge concluded, the fight finished, there is only silence. The sitting in the tent afterwards, trying to pray, trying to reconcile the ferocity of the encounter with justice, mercy, love. A soldier knows not only fear; he also knows, utterly, the theology of fact. He knows there can be no formed or secure judgements about the nature of what happens. He may later, when the abrupt brutality of fighting is past, pretend to some claim of righteousness, but while he is part of the actual momentary activity of conflict, no such thoughts can enter in. He experiences the total theology of event, where there is no thought, no calculation of the relativity of merit as pertaining to this or that course of action: there is just the headlong rush, the raised arm, the strike, the enemy's face, the smell of powder, guts, excrement. This is the venture that gives us the opportunity of earning a reputation for valour.

Forget the poets. Their attention is always fixed on some object other than event. It can be a benefice to be gained from authority; the likelihood (increasing perhaps as the facility for flattery increases) of ennoblement; the allure of land, or of a position in the court; or that most harmful of all self-indulgences, the expansion of vanity at the expense of honour. But mostly, if they are any good, poets attach their interest only to one object: the exercise of the art of language through the airy labyrinths of which they glide without thought. To that extent they vye with the soldier, as he, too, must drive through the labyrinth of choosing without thought. But the man of arms makes his drive through immediate risk and consequence, whereas the poet moves through his field of understanding with some form of assurance that what he says is suspended in a mood of deferral, which can be, and often is, endlessly sustained. Neither soldier nor poet knows what he does, but the man at arms faces outcomes there and then. Forget the poets. Unless they take up arms and follow the soldier's trade.

The displays of the bards here in Munster have been a disgrace to behold. An O'Daly came to the Sheriff's house in Cork in the last fortnight, having heard that Lord Mountjoy was staying there, offering to trace my lineage back to Noah. This was the message brought to me as I sat in my room at the hour of four o'clock, looking out on to the muddy street that runs from the north to the south bridge. My humours have been in a discontented state for months now, and I have ague continually, and fever. I was lost in thinking of my condition, and worried about my health, which I am inclined to do when not engaged upon some project of action. There were no directions from London, and increasing rumours of the Queen's indisposition. My letters to Cecil were going mostly un-answered, and when he did decide to reply he wrote only the most perfunctory things, conveying the good wishes of Her Majesty and wishing me a healthful rest after my exertions at Kinsale. The street outside offered no diversion from the poi-sonous melancholy that steals over me in days of inaction. The nasal tones of the people outside, speaking some version of English steeped in archaic and vicious (and, I suspect, Danish) uses were an oppression to the spirit, so when the news came to me I thought the bard might be a diversion.

When he came in I regretted immediately my decision. He strode over to me, where I sat by the leaded window, and straightaway sank to his knees and bowed his head. He said, in English that showed some signs of education, that this was the greatest honour in his life, to be in the presence of a famous warrior and knight. I looked down on the thick black hair of his bent head, and noticed that his hands, folded reverently in front of him, were carefully manicured. I told him to get up and to sit opposite me in the window alcove, and to say what he had come to say. He raised himself, sat back into the seat and, closing his eyes, began to recite, in a curious shifting drone, a long farrago of nonsense connecting Blount with someone he called Blanid, some amazon of the ancient lore of their damned country. He then went on, in a hurtling mono-tone, his head to one side, eyes shut as if possessed by the incan-tation he was uttering, to say that she, in her tragic death (something about falling or being pushed off a clifftop in Munster) would now be revenged by her doughty offspring (me!), whose valour was dedicated to cleansing Ireland of the impurities of inherited guilt.

The only difference between this effusion and those tendered in London to the powerful was in the pretence of total sincerity with which this one was purveyed. And enthusiasm. This O'Daly was seemingly wracked by that ancient wrong and when he finished his tirade he opened his eyes, and I saw to my disgust that the wretch was weeping with emotion. I told him to get out, but he begged me to allow him to stay while he composed himself; and also said that if his ode did not please me to the extent of my wishing to make a contribution in recognition of his narrative powers, then he might have some factual matters that could elicit a more favourable response.

I told him to speak plainly. Did he wish to inform on someone? Had he information he wanted to sell? Dry-eyed now, he nodded. Yes. I told him to proceed and to come to the point at issue swiftly. He insisted, however, that the wandering preamble composed of all that nonsensical and odious lore was germane to what he now wished to impart. He said that his genealogical sources revealed to him (and here he stopped portentously, letting the silence build) that I was the one destined to cleanse the wounds of this distressed country of his: that I was its redeemer. And that what he had to say would reveal to me where my duties lay and the path I had to take. I begged him once more to come to the point. I shall try to give here something of his own garbled wordage in this account, because the manner of the recitation in its mixture of ignorance and rodomontade only heightened for me the outrage I felt at what was being purveyed, and my anger at he who had brought the tale.

'The damage, most honoured sir, is done every day, almost, at the place of the boar's head: Kanturk. There meets there a colloquy of rhymers whose toy is to rhyme enemies to death. One of their number claims to have as his familiar Nicholas of Cusa; another claims nightly visitations from Eriugena, the philosopher of Charles the Bald. Yet another says he met at Oxford one Giordano Bruno, and it is he, my lord, who damages you.'

These were tiresome mimicries of the frivolous paganism of Marlowe and his ilk in London. But there was a jangling of my nerves when I heard the name of Bruno. I asked him to proceed. Who was this Oxonian?

'This man, your most gracious honour, has studied at Salamanca. His insouciance is not to be borne. He calumniated me with the MacCarthy Mór himself. He is a churl, sir; a man plastered in bog mire who pretends to learning. All his thinking converts to rot. His mind can hold thought only as a cow's hide holds lumps of dried turd. His words spill out of his mouth with the lack of discrimination of a bowl of porridge regurgitated. And he is held, and holds himself, in high regard. Now when this school of malice convenes, which they do every week, their confabulations lasting through the night, each one in turn declares a malediction, comprising a various mixture of scorn, taunt, defamation, insult, calumny. Such is the sedition of their fellowship in this guild of hate that each unites his passion to that of the incantator, so that, they believe, an enchantment is worked upon the victim. Your honour was, last week, the victim of the Oxonian and this tribe of malefactors.'

I asked him who this man was and what was said.

'You may know, your honour, that we, those of us in the bardic craft, are trained in the arts of memory, but I have only heard this recital once, and that from an imperfect source, in that he was not there in Kanturk when this man, whose name I will in a moment vouchsafe, your honour, gave forth. Before I name him there is the customary fiscal reward.'

I asked him how much he wanted and learned that there was to be separate payments for the man's name, and for the words of his calumny. I asked for the total price, and he named it as one hundred gold pieces. At this I laughed out loud, and looked down at the street below the window. A woman was standing on the paving opposite, holding a tray of wizened apples, held by a string around her neck. Apart from her, the street was almost empty, trade having greatly diminished in the recent disturbances. I wondered at the power of money: it had her out there on the street, and I here in Ireland at war, and this miserable wretch O'Daly before me engaged on the most intimate, careful and studied act of betrayal. I agreed to pay the money to him, and asked him to name my calumniator.

'His name, sir, is O'Dwyer, an O'Dwyer of the Glen, up in County Tipperary. Matthew is his given name. His people, close allies to the wild and inchoate Condons, to whom they are bound in the close relations of dependence and the mutuality fosterage brings, are rebels like their traditional landowners, the Condons, are. You will recall, sir, the massacres and degradation enacted some years ago, following the efforts of Her Gracious Majesty to civilise Munster, in those areas north of Mitchelstown, the valleys and fastnesses between the

Knockmealdown Mountains and the Galtees. The people behind these outrages were, in many cases, O'Dwyers and Condons, sometimes acting separately, sometimes in close consort. This civil malignity, continued over generations, has in Matthew O'Dwyer's case been further whetted by his time at Salamanca, then Oxford, in which latter place he proceeded under the false name of Matthew Glen, proclaiming himself an ardent convert to the reformed faith of the English Church. There, schooling himself in the disciplines of logic, philosophy and mathematics, he added to his innate propensity to rebellion an active and luxuriating intelligence. All of which is, I think, evident in the outrageous audacity and trickery of this defamation of you.'

I asked him what this was. I found my stomach contracting with tension. The world of words and rumour terrifies me, mainly because I know that there is no one who, should his secrecies be published to the world at large, would not be disgraced. There are no just men. That is why I am a soldier.

'The recitation of your faults proceeded not without much preamble, detailing your lineage (inexactly, of course: my version is the truth). And then it came to the point of shame. O'Dwyer's verses, in an elaborate metre full of jokes and trickery, short lines and curt rhymes interweaving with longer more sonorous declarations, went on to state, explicitly, that you, sir, with the royal knight Sir Philip Sidney, committed sodomy on the night before Zutphen.'

I look at this grey face before me, in the light of the window. I wanted to tear his features open.

I recalled the night before the battle at Zutphen. We were worn out by skirmishes with the Spaniards over the previous months. They had, at that time, reduced the art of warfare to a frivolous and irksome baiting. There would be a night-raid against an encampment outside Flushing; I or Sidney would go and investigate, and we'd find one or two people killed, and no sign of where the Spaniards had got to, or why they had made the incursion. We knew it was a tactic employed to unsettle us, to jangle our attention with fear and suspense. Sidney decided to make a strike against them, and when he heard that the Spanish-occupied town of Zutphen was to be supplied he decided to mount an ambush on it himself. He asked me to be with him on the assault and I agreed. We encamped the night before outside of Zutphen with a small force of trusted men. He and I retired together to our tent, where we spent the night revolving in our conversation affairs of state and also the heart, during which Sidney spoke to me very honestly about his mistress and of the connivance of her husband Lord Rich in their passion. All knew of Rich's accommodation with his wife, and all knew it was for his own advancement. Sidney said that Rich was no better than a pander of Troy or a pimp of Ephesus; and I know now, to my own cost and heartache, how true this was. Rich's agile temperament moves to whatever emotional attachment may seem an advantage. Even now he writes me private letters, lauding my zeal and energy in the Irish campaign, hoping, needless to say, that whatever advancement I may procure out of these dire passages may also, through the conduit of his pimpery, flow to him. These matters occupied Sidney and I for the best part of the night.

Towards morning we spoke about poetry and its relations to practical knowledge and the pressures of state. He, as ever, called for a new world to be revealed through the effort of verse; I, more cautiously, and with far less assurance and learning, expressed a preference for a poetry steeped in the roughness of experience. This way we kept our minds and passions true before the encounter next day. I do not doubt that this man was one of the most estimable ever, and that his fame will always shine brightly in the annals of England.

The next day all our anticipation and calculation went amiss. We were in bad order; our prior directives and commands had not taken account of the circumstance that would arise if the enemy were disposed separately with outriders and guards as well as the main column. The many impotent skirmishes of the past months led us to rely too much on the effect of an impetuous charge. As soon as we saw them coming across the flat plain towards the town Sidney roared at me as he drove his mount fiercely forward.

He was galloping straight at them, and far ahead of the rest of us. They were well-armed with their guns prepared, which they discharged at him. He was not hit, even though he rode through their line, flailing about him with his sword. Still unhurt, he wheeled his horse about and rode back through them again, while we were now engaged in fighting the guards and outriders that had ridden up to divert our following charge. I saw Sidney turn again and face back into the main column. A Spaniard with a huge firepiece dismounted his horse, and stood, legs apart, to take careful aim at Sidney as he was hurtling back into the press of men. There was a vast and awful report, and the marksman discharged his weapon at Sidney at a range of no more than a few yards. The horse gave out a fiercesome shrieking bleat. When the smoke cleared I saw Sidney riding back towards us, forcing his mount onwards. When he came up close I saw that his leg had been shattered. The thigh bone and the knee were visible in the mixture of human and animal gore. The horse slumped dead.

The Spaniards, taking advantage of our shock at the terrible wounding of our leader, made off to the safety of the town, the column still intact. Sidney did not recover from this wound, and died in a matter of days.

This was the man that Matthew O'Dwyer, from somewhere in the bogs and fens of the mountains of Tipperary, was traducing along with me. There was little possibility that O'Daly was lying: the circumstances of O'Dwyer's stay at Oxford, the knowledge he would have gleaned there concerning Sidney and his friendship with me, allowed him to create and broadcast villainy. This man had to be punished. I asked O'Daly where he was to be found.

'You'll find him, your honour, in his native haunts up in Tipperary, in the Glen of Aherlow.'

O'Daly withdrew, after making protestations of service and loyalty, and left me sitting in the embrasure, thinking of the futility of life in this execrable country. Where misprision awaits every action, where the only emotion the natives are capable of is anger, where hate governs all. These conditions infect us and we become like them in word and deed and thought. I resolved to go to Tipperary, find this O'Dwyer, and kill him. I would kill him on the way to Dublin. The messengers were out around the country doing their work, telling everyone that this time I might be prepared to accept a submission from O'Neill and that northern crew of adulterers and insurgents. Suggesting, too, that I might be prepared to meet him somewhere outside the Pale around Dublin. Meanwhile, my worry is the state of health of Her Gracious Majesty.

1903

MARY O'DWYER

I decided to go up onto the deck when the word went round that we were coming up to Dunkettle Bridge. I leaned against the railings and looked over towards Glanmire, and at the dark stretch of water beyond the bridge. The tide was out, so the sloblands alongside the river were visible in the soft grey sameness. The rain slanted down. I could feel the coldness of the rail pressing against my slightly swollen stomach. I was now three months gone and hardly showing.

I couldn't stick it any longer with Jim in Leeds, so I came back to have the baby, disgrace or no disgrace. I don't know how it was I didn't cotton on sooner to what was going on, but then his nature is so free and easy it's impossible to get at what he's really thinking or feeling about anything.

I'll never forget that afternoon. I'd gone out to see if I could get an interview for a job in a solicitor's office in North Lane in Headingley, leaving Jim behind sitting at the kitchen table, no shirt on, braces over his bare slim chest, peeling the spuds for the dinner. He wasn't due back on the trams until seven, so we'd planned to eat at five thirty. I'd put three chops (two for him) in the meatsafe. I didn't tell him where I was going; I didn't want to raise any hopes. The clerking job was advertised in that morning's *Yorkshire Post*, saying that applicants should apply 'in person or in writing'. It would be worth having a job even for the few months before which it would become impossible to hide my condition. And who knows; I might find a decent kind of an employer who'd offer to take me back after, if I could arrange a minder for the baby. Then a house, a garden, calm Sunday dinners with the windows open in summer, Jim opposite me, smoking.

I said to Jim I wanted to go into town to see if I could lay my hands on some curtaining for the bare back window of the flat, and to get some almonds for a pudding I wanted to make. He took hardly any notice of me, just sitting there, peeling the potatoes, carefully ensuring that he was removing as little of the flesh as possible.

It was the beginning of spring, and walking down the Shire Oak Road I got the faint smell of the daffodils in the air, so plentiful were they in the gardens. I touched the old stone wall, I remember, and it was slightly warm. Even though the Leeds air was thick with dust and the stink of smelting iron, and a clammy mist from the cotton mills darkened even sunny days, somehow that afternoon, as I walked down the Shire Oak, the slight wind was fresh in a way that reminded me of walks out Bishopstown on Sundays when I was a child. I walked past a Jewish bakery, and smelled the yeasty breath that rolled out of its open door. But when I got to the solicitor's office it was closed and shuttered, with a sign up behind the slatted blind

and blue pane of glass. I wondered if I should go into town
anyway, but decided against it: it might be a rush to get home
and prepare the food for five thirty, so I went back to the flat.

Climbing the stairs, I heard something I never again want to
hear: the animal howls of a woman in pleasure, which sound
for all the world as if someone is torturing her. It was a bleak
piercing sound, not that loud, but pained and intimate and
fiercely jarring. I didn't know then what was going on. I
thought someone had been hurt. I pushed open the door of
the flat, which had been left slightly ajar, and then I saw something which burned the eyes out of my head. The landlady,
who was aged about forty-five or so, but who I always
thought had a presentable figure, was sitting on Jim's lap,
naked from the waist down, legs to each side of him. She was
still wearing her hat, I saw, in a kind of horrified trance noticing the slightest details. It was a blue pillbox affair, with a veil
even, which she had pushed back. She was pushing her face
against his, which I couldn't see, and had him caught by the
hair with her gloved hands. She rolled slightly and I saw that
she had him inside her. For a few seconds they didn't notice me
and I watched them excite themselves more and more, as he
drove into her and they approached their climax. The potato
peelings were behind them on the table.

Then Jim moved his head and saw me, but by now they
were so far gone they were like dogs and couldn't stop. He
(and I'll never forget this, never) he just closed his eyes and
gave a few last shoves, she moaning his name all the time, then
finished.

She turned around to see me standing there, and then said:
'Oh Mrs Condon. I'm sorry', and began to giggle first, then
to laugh uproariously, shamelessly standing in front of me,
swabbing herself with a handkerchief she'd pulled out of her
glove.

'Look, Mary, what harm?' said Jim. 'Let's not get upset
about this. We can all of us, you and me and Jenny, have a fine
old time if we're sensible and not too ready to blame or to

make accusations.'

I couldn't believe what I was hearing.

'Yes,' said the landlady, a Mrs Liversedge. Who now I was supposed to call 'Jenny'. 'This is the twentieth century we're in. No one takes any notice. Why don't we just be adult and grown up about this. You and I, Mary' – this to me, with a wink – 'can have our tea with Jim, then go down to the Shire Oak and have a drink while we wait for him to come back from work. No need to be greedy.'

'No,' I said, as calmly as I could, 'I'm not a whore like you. I'm going home this very night and you're welcome to him, with your fancy hat, your gloves, and your bare arse. How long have you been at this? Not that it matters now.'

'We've been lovers,' said the landlady, coyly now sitting up on the table and taking no trouble to make herself the least respectable, 'more or less since you arrived. Within a week, I'd say, we'd discovered our mutual interest.' Laughing as she said this.

'You can't go back to Cork. What'll you do?' asked Jim.

'Don't you mind about that.'

I went into the bedroom, packed my few things and took the train to Fishguard. I still had much of Holmes's money, even after paying the hotel bill at the Queen's and our few weeks in Leeds.

It was early morning when the boat docked at the harbour in Cork. I watched the jettymen catch the huge ropes and slip them over the curiously shaped iron mooring bollards, like giant anvils riveted to the quayside's heavy stone. As I looked at their solid bulk, I felt a tiny stir inside me, and thought it was comforting, the intimate knowledge that I had of this other life I was carrying. What will it be like for him or her? Will he or she be a traveller? What will whatever it is be like? A person full of fear, like I'm in danger of becoming; or someone reckless and strong, totally unabashed in front of others?

I walked up the quay, feeling protected by this secret, inside, a kind of power, even though to anyone taking a common-sense look at my situation, I was in the deepest trouble. I decided to head for Fat Mag's out in Rathcooney, where, I hoped, there would be no judgements on me. I took a horse and trap at Parnell Place, the driver agreeing to take me out to Rathcooney for two shillings.

Fat Mag, an unmarried aunt, my father's sister, lived alone in a house she'd inherited from an uncle on her mother's side, my paternal grandmother, that is. For some reason, I know, and have always known, who everybody is on each side of the O'Dwyers: who the first, second, third cousins are; the once, and twice, and third removed, the relation by blood, and their different responsibilities to each other. I don't even have to work these things out. I know them. Just as I knew now, I hoped, that Fat Mag would react as I imagined she would at the news I was going to bring in the door to her.

There she was, as I always found her when I visited, sitting to one side of her large fire with its barred grate, turning the bellows' handle in its circular motion, a pipe stuck in her tooth-less mouth, her other hand, brown from work and turf, resting on her overall. She looked at me as I came through the half-door, squinting against the light.

'How are you girl? Sit down. I heard you were in trouble. Are you well? I thought you had taken the boat.'

'I had Auntie Mag. But I'm back. I ran off with a man who was worse than the one I left behind.'

'There's not born yet,' she said, moving her soft lips into a slightly comical expression, all the more striking because her chin and lower jaw and upper lip were fairly thickly covered with hair, 'a man worthy of any woman. *Any* woman. And there's certainly none to compete with you, the pride of the O'Dwyers.'

I wept and she reached out a warm hand to touch my face.

'Don't fret,' she said, 'it'll be fine. You always have a place to stay here. I never judge anyone, you know that. And I can, if you want, see about getting rid of the little creature. Poor little thing.'

'No,' I said. 'No. Elliott Holmes offered that as well. No. This is my own child.'

'I hope,' she said, 'it's worthy of the sacrifice you're making. Most children aren't, to my way of thinking. But then I'm no one to be offering advice.'

1874

PATSY CONDON

Mr Klein was rolling up the bales of cloth displayed outside his tailor's shop on small trestles. During the day he'd wait inside the glass-panelled door until someone would happen along, and, taken by a colour or design, would finger the cloth, then out he'd come, all enthusiasm and conviction about the quality, value, durability, and so on, of the piece of cloth that had taken the eye of the passer-by.

'Evening, Mr Klein. You're packing in early today,' said Patsy Condon.

'That's so, Mr Condon, but we must prepare for Passover, and I want the young boy to be ready with his answers and responses to the prayers. And I don't want any hesitation. His grandmother and uncles will be there, and he must keep up the family name. But he's a good boy, Samuel is.'

'Yes,' said Patsy. 'I hope you have a very happy celebration.'

'And you?' said Klein. 'What of you?'

'A little music in the shop, and then perhaps a visit to my daughter's.'

'Ah yes,' said Klein. 'Family. It makes us slaves to chance, but it frees us from the world, too. It gives us another way of looking at people. When you consider that they come from families, too, not unlike your own.'

'People are the same the world over, Mr Klein. The same good-hearted idiots; the same vengeful twisters.'

'Let us not darken our thoughts at this holy time of the year, Mr Condon. Let us not darken our thoughts. Here. Take this for Maureen.' He handed him a bale end of blue curtaining, with a recurring floral device in deep indigo.

'Thank you. Happy Easter.'

He walked up the pavement to his shop, Condon's Music Emporium, with its name on a low-hung awning, beneath which a straggle of people were gathered looking at the instruments. He went and stood amongst them and listened to their comments on the violins in their cases, trombones inverted on stands, trumpets, tenor and flugel horns, a harp to the rear of the display, and in front, dominating all, a German grand piano in black wood. Though he was on a side street off Fifth Avenue, he now ran one of the biggest music shops in New York.

He went inside. It was late afternoon, and he felt refreshed after the coffee which he always took at this time at the drugstore round the corner of the avenue with the day winding down. He surveyed the racks of sheet music, the big folios of symphonies, and the flimsier leaflets of popular songs. He loved this place, with its atmosphere of elegance and relaxation. It still amazed him and terrified him not a little that it was possible for such as he to make a living, indeed to become moderately rich, selling things that were of no practical use to anyone. Music? Entertainment, passing the time. And yet he remembered nights out in Kildorrery and Kilworth when, as he played, he felt that all those listening to him fiddling away on his gimcrack violin were involved in something that bound them all together. Of course he had had that help from other quarters as well, always gently tendered, but always the sense, too, that they could count on his assistance whenever it was required. O'Dowd had a very light touch.

Walking into his office, where he'd had a display case made for the instrument he'd carrried with him to Queenstown, then across the sea, he thought of one night in particular, at Kilbeheny crossroads. He sat down at his desk, the memo pad in front of him. He made a few idle strokes with his pencil. The face of old Ó Catháin came back to him: Ó Catháin, one of the greatest singers of Munster, with his long black hair and china blue eyes, which he closed when he raised his head to sing, blind into the air. There was total silence, only the snapping of wood in the fire. Ó Catháin sang a lament of a young girl for her drowned lover, and as his voice broached the terrible particulars of the song – the crabs at the sockets of his eyes, the eels infiltrating his flesh – his singing expanded into the words, forcing the audience to encounter the shock of them. There was a curving wail of passionate realisation as the harshness of male grief broke over the high and delicate movements of the voice. When he finished he opened his eyes and looked down at the hand holding his hat on his knee. Lifting it up high over his head he flung it to the floor beneath his feet and shouted: 'I'll live for ever.' A roar of approval from the company greeted this outburst.

Patsy smiled, remembering the thatched roof, the semidark, the pulse of excitement in the room. And then he thought of his daughter, out in the district of Queen's in a fine new house with her now better-behaved husband, her three children, Robert, Anthony and Ellen. Or Roberto, Antonio and Elena, as their father called them.

There was a knock at the door, and his secretary showed in
Pearse Condon, a distant relative living in Utica, New York
State, originally from Ballymacoda at the mouth of the Black-
water river, down from Youghal. He'd come in for the music
that evening at the shop, but was earlier than the rest. Pearse
Condon's poems and songs were widely known amongst the
New York Irish, who greatly enjoyed his manic and unpredict-
able humour, his black wide-brimmed hats, his dandified behaviour and his jaunty walk.

Others soon came: O'Brien, the police chief, with his fiddle;
the piper Doran, who had a job in the sanitary department; the
flautist McConnell, a journalist; the lawyer McPhelimey, who
also played the fiddle; and many more. Soon there were
twenty or so in the room. After drink was poured Patsy took
up his fiddle and began 'O'Neill's March'. All joined in, and
soon the room was full of the driving hope and energy of the
tune: mountain passes came before their eyes, valleys, the sea,
the enemy dead.

Then Condon from Ballymacoda moved to the centre of the
floor and began, in Irish, a mock-heroic declaration:

In the blackest of the black blacknesses that was known as
1847, save that there were other blacknesses, too, but
none could beat that black for perfect black. The black
that only black can understand. Well, in that black the
Aeneas of the Irish, Pearse Condon, wiry and slight,
began a voyage that will break the scruple of every maid
from Dunseverick to Baltinglass and points further south.
It was then that this Aeneas took upon himself the burden
of the relief of the United States of America, and resolved
to stow away on board the schooner *Troy* by means of
installing himself in a mackerel barrel, head above the
pickled fish. This he did, and they set sail from Youghal
harbour. Zephyrus and all the other winds, cheeks puffed,
blew the ship first down to the Azores and then out into
mid-Atlantic, way off course. Pearse Condon's belly was

now beginning to become gaseous, with his diet solely the pickled fish that were his element. His tongue had grown so long from stretching out to catch the moisture off the barrel's slats benights (he'd not lift the covering lid by day and he was too scared to leave his barrel at night) that he could touch his Adam's apple with it if he wished. One night, when he was licking the black drops off the seepage on the planks, someone grabbed him by the pliant member. It was so black he couldn't see who it was but a female voice announced that it was none other than Aoibheall of Craig Liath, the Munster goddess herself, come to ask his aid in a dispute with Conán Maol Mac Mórna. So tender was her touch on his sensitive organ that he could not refuse, and then before he knew it he was whisked out of the barrel with a plop, then with another plop he was taken underwave. He felt the ocean streaming through his hair. Thank God, he thought, I was badly in need of a wash after all those weeks in a mackerel barrel. So then, with another plop, they landed up on a broad swerving beach, with the foamy water necklacing the golden strand with white. As they came out of the water he stole a glance at his fairy companion. She was white as air, white as the milk of spring, white as the soft fur on the belly of a hare. She strode through the water, with firm and muscular thighs, the likes you'd see on a young blacksmith. He admired her gait, and the way her hair streamed in her wake along the silvery waves. And there stood Conán before them: bald and hairy-chested; fat and yellow; smiling and toothless.

'Now,' sez he to Aoibheall, 'have you got someone to defend your virtue?'

'This man,' sez she.

'Fine out,' sez he.

And he flung a knife at Condon, but our Pearse was wiry and slight, as I said, and he ducked. Conán made a rush at him, and knocked him down into the foam. They rolled about in the water, but Conán got the better of Pearse and took him by the throat, and started to strangle the life out of him. Pearse's mouth opened in agony as Conán's steely grip grew tighter, and his tongue came out as he gagged. Conán had not seen anything as horrific ever in his life; the long sinuosity of it, its musculous dexterity, its powers of probe and extension. Conán thought it was some kind of serpent growth attached to his opponent, a secret weapon like the Gae Bolg of Cú Chulainn, and he ran off down the beach screaming. He was so scared he became the patch on the arse of a sailor's working trousers.

Meanwhile, Pearse and the lady lived for ever in her land, eating only scallops and lamb's tongues, and drinking only mead and the purest water. Pearse never again ate salt the rest of his days. In time his tongue returned back to normal, and he always kept it civil in his head.

After this Patsy opened up the music again with 'Mná na hÉireann' – women of Ireland. As they drifted through the first bars he saw, with pleasure, his old friend the Fenian Fergal O'Dowd come through the door. He waved with his bow.

1904

JIM CONDON

There was a light tap on the door. I hoped it was Jenny, the landlady, calling to be 'serviced', as she described it. This all was a new experience for me, because never before had I come across a woman who enjoyed doing it so much. She'd ask for what she wanted, and she'd be very exact about it, too, saying where she wanted to be touched, and how. I enjoyed the thrill of this, and when I'd be driving the tram my mind would stray off to recall what she'd whispered or did during our last session together. She had me half crazy with desire, and I hardly stopped thinking of her. When I got home in the afternoon there was the tension of wondering if she'd come up to the flat today, which she mostly did, although sometimes she had to attend to her husband if he was at home. Mostly though, he was away, a commercial traveller whose job took him off for three days at a time or more, visiting Hull, or Darlington, or Sheffield. He was a lingerie salesman, and covered all of the Ridings of Yorkshire for his company. I needn't say that Jenny took great pleasure in wearing his products, and in letting me see her in them and out of them.

This daze I was in, day to day, dulled any memory I had of the shame I felt over what had happened with Mary O'Dwyer. When it would come into my mind I'd find myself cursing to myself under my breath. My face burned when I thought of the look she gave me when she turned and went out of the room. I don't think I've ever been ashamed of something I'd done in my life before. It was a terrible feeling, one that agitated me in my stomach, and I still end up with pains in my legs if I allow myself to think on that moment for too long. Shame can exhaust you, something I'd not realised. If it weren't for Jenny, I think this shame might have made me seriously ill, and might even have killed me. Is it possible to die of shame? But luckily Jenny's eagerness and her sexy tricks kept those thoughts from my mind a good part of the time at least. I suppose I must be a very coarse type of person: I don't seem to mind much what happens to me or to others, as long as I'm occupied. But this Mary O'Dwyer business was different.

'Is that you, Jenny?' I asked, when I heard the light tap. Although she normally would just turn the knob and walk in bold as brass, lifting her skirt with a flounce. Another knock. I went to the door and opened it. Outside stood a youth of about sixteen, with a closely cropped head, dressed in a grubby black suit, and twisting in his hands a large black cap. The tips of his upright shirt collar were stained with coal dust.

'Mr Condon, sir?'

I nodded.

'Mr O'Dowd, Mr Fergal O'Dowd wants to see you over in

Chapeltown, this evening at seven o'clock. In the Roundhay Bar. He says it's very urgent, sir.'

'Fine. OK I'll be there,' I said.

What did O'Dowd want with me? He had got me the job on the tramway because he seemed to be able to exercise a good deal of power in crucial areas, although he had no official post anywhere in Leeds that I knew of. He was a union man, and he was on the fringe of the labour movement. He wasn't involved in politics, but he could influence housing allocations by lobbying councillors or the mayor's office. He did not seem to have any source of income and yet he was never short of money. He had spent time in the States and was a man now in his sixties or even seventies, but he walked with the speed and briskness of a youth. He drank heavily in pubs up the York Road and in Chapeltown, but was never drunk. He had the reputation of a fighter, and was, it was said, still in contact with the American Fenians, who sent him money. He was a figure that people talked about and feared. He spoke in a low tone, scarcely moving his lips, and he held your gaze while he talked, seeming never to close those small eyes. I wasn't looking forward to meeting him. He made one feel, always, somewhat useless. Power in men, I think, is gained by making others experience fear, and that was what he induced in me: fear.

I took the tram over to Chapeltown for the meeting with O'Dowd, and after I entered the half-empty bar I saw him standing at the counter, back to the door and leg up on the footrest, motionless. He saw me in the mirror and turned.

'Condon, what'll you have?'

When the drinks were ready he nodded towards a seat in a dark recessed booth. As we slid along the bench I felt a thrust of fear: a surge of anxiety from my groin up to my chest.

He sat opposite me, calmly eyeing me over his refreshed pint of bitter. 'You know why I want to talk to you.'

'No.'

'That was not a question.'

'No?'

'I'm saying it again, for the last time.' He slowed his speech and gently but firmly placed a silence between each syllable. 'You know why I want to talk to you.'

I realised that somehow he'd come to know about Mary. I answered, 'Yes.'

'Well. We can get on now. What are you going to do about the O'Dwyer girl?'

'Why are you asking me that question? I had nothing to do with the condition she's in.'

'No, but it's common knowledge amongst us here that you looked after her when she needed it. And that was well and good, more than many a man would do. But then for you to treat her the way any thug would treat a woman in trouble, only makes things worse. A bad act following a good one only destroys the good. You owe it to yourself, boy, to try to be consistent.'

'Fair enough, but you should be talking to Morgan Holmes, her so-called boss, and his father who tried to buy her off. So much for the merchant princes of Cork.'

'Don't think for a moment that they will get away with anything. But it's you that I'm concerned about now. You and your disgraceful behaviour.'

'May I ask, Fergal, with the greatest respect, why it is that you are concerning yourself about what is a private matter?'

'It's not a private matter when the honour of an Irishman is shown to be lacking. And in any case, the Condons and I are obliged to each other from way back. Let me explain to you a little about this. I want to make you understand how seriously I take this, and how I will not stop until I can persuade you to do the right thing. Years ago a man called Patsy Condon came to me in New York looking for help. His daughter was being abused by a boyfriend and I was asked to see to it that he was stopped. He was an Italian, and what they called a runner for the Organization over there in Little Italy. I spoke to his bosses, they spoke to him – in fact they took him and beat the living shite out of him in an alley behind a café he was eating in one night – and he changed his behaviour. He married the girl and they had a lovely family. Years later I asked Patsy Condon to return the favour. I asked him to look after someone for a week or so. He did it, and did it many times after. We advanced him money, he prospered, and when he died a very old man, ten, fifteen years ago, he was one of the wealthiest Irishmen in New York, and his grandchildren professors and accountants. You, Condon, have the same blood as this man, and I will never see that name being disgraced without taking steps to stop it. That is what I am doing now. Here, take this.' He dug deep into a pocket inside his waistcoat and pulled out a thick wad of notes. He peeled off five – twenty-five pounds. 'This is yours. Do the right thing. It's all that's left. It's all that you'll be able to remember with any pride. That a few times, at least, you did the right thing when it would have been easier to have done nothing. Take my word for it. Take the money. Go home and marry this girl. You'll have your troubles, but don't all of us? And as long as I live I'll be your friend.'

He reached out a hand and put it on my shoulder. I wept in relief and in astonishment at the fact that I'd discovered something I didn't think I could ever have. A sense of honour.

1753

EOGHAN MacCARTHY

THE POET MacCARTHY WRITES IN CARRIGNAVAR, NEAR CORK, OF
EVENTS AT THE TIME OF THE DEATH OF THE QUEEN OF ENGLAND,
ELIZABETH THE FIRST, WITH A PREAMBLE OF HIS OWN STATE
AND THAT OF THE COUNTRY IN HIS TIME.

Now is a time of great tribulation over all of Munster and in
the generality of Ireland. These woes, to which we have now
grown accustomed, afflict us no less for all that we are
becoming the jibe of Europe for our melancholy and
continuous plaint. I turn my own hand now, with the greatest
difficulty, to scribing in this foreign language, soon to be our

only means of survival and support. And I am writing this not even knowing if there is anyone to read these halting records, for my companions daily are illiterate in both Irish and English, and can scarcely comprehend anything of the latter, save the most rudimentary commands and injunctions. Not long ago, less than a decade even, all Munster was in a state of high exaltation. Scarcely a rich man's house of the Irish did not have a weekly visitant informing him of the latest news from France. The expectation was high that the Stuart prince would come ashore in Kerry or the wild coast of Cork off Durrus or Allihies. No matter that the long-awaited arrival was deferred continually, these messengers came to the houses of our strong farmers and small Catholic gentry carrying the certainty that our liberator was at hand. Now all know how vain this expectation was.

I cannot think how this country can ever prosper: its leadership is astray; there is growing daily a new desperation amongst the people which heartless men will carefully exploit. There has been no leader of our people for more than a hundred years, and there can be no prospect of any man arising who can bring us now into governable unity and accord. I can see, although I must be careful to admit that I have very little ability to penetrate the heart of state, no other course of affairs than that those who now wield this authority over us will continue to do so, and while they may temper their harshness by conciliatory acts of kindness from time to time, these will only make us, those whom they govern, more conscious of their ascendancy. So does the simple act of charity become an art of injustice in a system which operates by means of, and thereby daily legitimates, dependency. The harassment of emotion which such a slighting enmity works makes the likes of me brood and rage, rage and brood. My fancy, too abrupt in imagining insult, betakes itself into a wild terrain of unspeakable anger, but it has no direction, it has no government, it has no leadership. The truth of the matter is my country craves leadership, a most dangerous affliction, for this role will most likely be usurped by scoundrels and malefactors time after time until we are permitted one just and careful man.

It is often argued by the religiously minded or the craven-hearted (it is often difficult to know which is which) that God will reward us for our sufferings; or that our sufferings are ordained by His divine grace for our betterment, and for the cleansing of our will and deeds. My own persuasion, although not held without the greatest hesitancy and doubt, is that the fate of the country or its people is not a matter that can be traced to divine agency; rather must its origin be found in the corrupt heart of English and Irish men and women. For myself, and in this perhaps I am heretical, I pray only because I know that Our Lord Jesus Christ cannot be held responsible for what men do. He offered himself in atonement for our wilful destruction of each other and of Him in us, but He was not responsible. How else could He make a sacrifice that was free and uncompelled?

But I am digressing. I sit down to record, in the condition of melancholy despair that now has all of the Catholic gentry of Ireland in its grip, events that occurred not far from here many years ago in the time of Elizabeth of England. It is a little-known encounter, but one that has always seemed to me to emblematise much of our difficulty. It concerns the great English general, the Earl of Devonshire, Charles Blount, Lord Mountjoy, famous as the illegitimate husband of the notorious mistress of Sir Philip Sidney, and the man who defeated Hugh O'Neill, the Fox of Tyrone, not by guile, but by sheer force of determination. A great English soldier, lauded by Samuel Daniel, court poet to the nobility of Britain.

Rumour was rife in the aftermath of the defeat of Kinsale. It was said that O'Neill had planned that defeat, that he wanted Mountjoy to pursue him north into the bleak acres of midland bog, and then lead him astray and destroy him in the ague-ridden foulness of the Irish winter. O'Donnell, who was in Spain, was said to be amassing another Armada, save that this time there would be a hundred thousand fully armed soldiers from Spain and Italy whose duty would be to restore the true faith to eminence in Ireland and in Britain. But Mountjoy did nothing. He sat calmly and waited, because he perceived, as an excellent commander of men always should, that the defeated, alone, will exhaust themselves in vain striving, dischoate action, and ungoverned thought. There was, however, one rumour that was brought to him by a member of the O'Daly learned family, which held it that he had committed, with Sidney, the sin of sodomy at Zutphen. This fabrication was concocted by one Matthew O'Dwyer, a young man educated in Salamanca and Oxford, who gained all the greater credence from his having been at the latter seat of learning. Mountjoy, when he learned this from the lips of O'Daly, resolved in his heart to take revenge.

He left Cork with a force of one hundred men, hand-picked and hardened soldiers. He was going to Dublin in any case, but for months he had shown no inclination to activity of any sort; now when he marched he did so with such precipitate speed that he was at Fermoy before the word spread on the streets of Cork that he had gone. Nor did any of the legion of spies that surrounded him know of his intent, for O'Daly had kept his counsel, so well had he been paid by Mountjoy.

By mid-afternoon he and his force arrived at the village of Barna. He stopped and dismounted in the tiny square of houses, dust-filled in the dry air from the hooves of a hundred horses. There was no one in sight, the villagers having mostly fled into the nearby woods and caves when they heard the pounding of this cavalcade of Mountjoy. Leather creaked on the harnesses of the horses, the men breathed heavily and harshly as the dust settled and they watched Mountjoy kick in one door after another. He arrived back out of one; stooping through the narrow door, he dragged a boy of about fourteen years behind him by his long hair. He threw him on the ground with his face in the dirt and rammed his foot into the boy's backside, holding him down with it and driving him along the ground at the same time, trying to keep his balance as he did so. He demanded to know where Matthew O'Dwyer the rebel was. The youth pleaded that he did not know where the gentleman lived, and that indeed (in as much as panic allowed him to form any semblance of speech) he did not know anyone of that name. Then Mountjoy hauled him up by his jerkin, and taking an arm in his hand he drew his sword and severed the limb at the wrist in one sweeping cut. The boy fell to the ground, confessed the whereabouts of O'Dwyer and begged forgiveness. The General hacked the boy to death with four or five cuts to the head.

Mountjoy, all records concur, rode with urgent force into the Aherlow Glen, making to where the fear-stricken youth had told him he would find his quarry. It was a place of mixed woodland and stone, with huge slabs of granite laid athwart each other around which a variegated forest of oak, aspen, rowan and beech grew in flourishing abundance. In the midst of this entangled demesne of rock and tree was the cave where O'Dwyer, a younger scion of his family and therefore expected to forage for himself in the wilds in the summer months, had made his usual court and encampment. Lord Mountjoy, taking no care of any kind to disguise his approach by stealth and therefore seeking none of the advantages of surprise, broke through the glossy leafage into the open space before O'Dwyer's lair.

There were twenty or so of the Irishman's retinue taking their leisure before the cave mouth, it being that time of the day when their main meal was over. The fires smoked heavily from the fat and the carcase residue that had been thrown on them after the repast. Mountjoy's rushing discomfitted them as they lay there in the air laden with grease, such that the English force was upon them before they scarcely had time to rise from the rocks covered with the rushes they reclined upon. With terrible dispatch most of O'Dwyer's followers were killed, the blades of the English swords making a harsh percussive music as steel cut through human meat and bone to clang against rock. But their chief, Lord Mountjoy, held back, to see if he could discern where O'Dwyer was. His hands trembled with rage and excitement as he sat on his mount, surveying the carnage before him in the smoking dale, now suffused with the odour of hot blood on stone. He saw a man walk calmly into the cave mouth, from the dark interior. He stood as if appraising the slaughter transpiring before his gaze, and then, with a kind of insouciant effrontery, he looked up at Mountjoy. The latter rode across to where the other stood and asked if he were O'Dwyer. The young man, as if careless of any danger, leaned against the wall of rock and looked to his feet and replied that there were many such present, that most of those his men were even now disporting themselves with were O'Dwyers.

Then Lord Mountjoy, upbraiding this youth for his insolence, told him who he was, that he was the Lord Deputy himself, and asked if he were the one who had calumniated him in Kanturk. O'Dwyer said that he never calumniated anyone, and that the worst invention could claim pertaining to Blount's reputation would never extend sufficiently to embrace the disgrace and shame he, Blount, should feel. Lord Mountjoy did not reply to this insult, but his soldiers, now desisting from their bloody labours, turned to look to see what he would do. His face was white. Slowly he dismounted, walked up to O'Dwyer, and took him by the locks of hair above his freckled face. He called for assistance and ordered his men to strip his enemy, and then proceeded to enact upon him, with his sword, that which O'Dwyer had said he and Sir Philip Sidney did at Zutphen. The young O'Dwyer, it is said, did not once give way to any exclamations of pain or implorings for mercy.

When I write this dismal account my thought is: how may such records free themselves from the attaints of accusation and remorse? I can see, years hence, many who will make the study of such atrocious deeds their sustenance and provender: I know there will be many whose goodness, darkened by rage, will rise from their writings, fangs dripping with saliva at the commital again of that which should be left unrecalled. Though I am a scribe, I grow ever more convinced that those who follow this wheedling trade deal dishonestly with history. Although not so culpable as those who style themselves historians who, with all the afflatus of circumstance and pomposity they seem to think such a title affords, nevertheless traffic in the material evidences of events with a liberty that assumes to itself a capacity to make fact accord with volition. When the actual material facts of a history are wretched in themselves it takes but little for those scribes and commentators who claim sincerity and justice as their guides to pervert entirely a condition already dismal to one of absolute ruin.

I lift my eyes and look out upon the fields of Carrignavar and feel, once more, that surge of love for this country that has animated all of us, good and bad, for so many years it is beyond telling.

THIS RECORD OF MISERY AND WOE
HEREIN INSCRIBED BY EOGHAN MacCARTHY
RELICT OF THE DRAGONS OF THE LEE
IN THE YEAR OF OUR LORD 1753

1930

NINA HOLMES

It was about ten years ago, maybe nine, that his drinking
began. He'd always liked a gin before his dinner, or perhaps a
light sherry, and he would, quite often, take claret with his
evening meal. I liked it when he drank a little; it lightened
him. He was always tense. But men are mostly like this. Tense.
Always either crowing about a gain or bemoaning a loss.
Never stable, never temperate.

I've always wanted to live in a temperate atmosphere, where
the light would fall on things in equanimity, and they would
come to your gaze affianced to each other in a steady calm. But
things were always irrupting: whether my father's screams of

agony in his study as he writhed on the floor in his last illness, his stomach ruined by whiskey; or the way I would, despite myself, keep noticing inanities of no consequence – such as the angle at which a matchbox lay on a table, or the smoke idling out from a cigarette in an ashtray. I am watchful, not that I want to be, but because I can never rid myself of the persuasion that what appears placid and settled in its decorum will shortly display an irreverent disregard for my expectations that things will stay as they are.

Morgan Holmes, when I was introduced to him at a cocktail party at the Royal Yacht Club in Crosshaven in, when was it? yes, summer 1904, seemed to have the steady composure of the satisfied man. He had a business, the family wholesale trade; he dressed well, and he was athletic and supple in his movements. I had noticed him that summer, in his yachting flannels, jump a five foot gap from the gunwale to quayside, rope in hand, to tie it round the bollard. I remember sitting looking at this man in white, full of energy, on the green lawn that extended from the club pavilion down to the moorings. I looked across at Curraghbinney's dark wood and felt happy. He was a man, and I felt glad, looking at him, that he and the likes of him were in the world. So that when I was introduced to him by my Uncle Stephen at the club a few weeks later, I had already begun to get excited when I thought of him. Which was a lot. It seemed as if I had nothing to do in the long days of summer. I was restless but enjoying my sense of bemused anticipation. I wasn't agitated in the way I had been back in Cappoquin during my father's illness, and afterwards, when he died.

My uncle was all kindness. I remember well the night he came into the drawing room in Cappoquin, where I was sitting at the small table in front of the window, trying to write a letter to an old school friend, trying to express something of how I felt after my poor jaded father's death. The words would not come; all there was in me was this huge feeling of hurt and anger and frustration. But I could put none of it down. I felt contempt for myself, my feelings, my thoughts, for words themselves, so arid and useless before me on the sheet of paper as I wrote. Every phrase that came to mind was a slack formula, a cliché, with no hint of the interior feeling of what it was like to be sitting there in the evening, staring out at the gravel, watching the tall rhododendrons swaying in the rain and wind. But when Stephen came in the atmosphere lightened.

I liked my uncle. Brisk and thoughtful at once, he had been a merchant seaman, and now owned a wine business in Cork, importing from Bordeaux and Oporto. He supplied my father with the crates of sherry, port and wine he had consumed with an ever-increasing appetite for self-destruction. Stephen had warned Father. I remember hearing him say, in an even, low tone, to my father at the bottom of the cellar stairs (I was in the hallway eavesdropping) that he didn't mind; as far as he was concerned he could drink as much as he liked, but well, he'd just like to point out that four cases of red wine a month was excessive: that worked out, he said, lightly, in a slightly jocular tone, of a case a week – two bottles a day. And that wasn't counting the gin and the whiskey, and the, well . . . 'You know yourself,' he said to Father. No reply. Silence from Father. The slow and heavy tread up the cellar steps, then him inviting Stephen into the library to sample a new fresh claret he'd just discovered. Young, lively, full of bounce, ha, ha. The harsh ironic laugh.

Stephen came to stay when Father died, and looked after all the funeral arrangements, as well as sorting out the estate. The evening he came to speak to me he had spent four days in the library going through Father's accounts, hardly speaking in the evening when we had supper together. When I'd ask him how things were he'd be non-commital and just shrug, but this night he came in, and he looked worn out.

'Nina,' he said. 'You're in a very poor situation, I'm sorry to say. It's not surprising, given your poor father's problems and his terrible and painful illness, but, according to my first calculations, when everything is added in, including the redemption of a massive mortgage with the Munster and Leinster Bank in Youghal, and unpaid wine bills to merchants other than myself, and all taxes and death duties, all you will have left will be a portion of the value of the house. You will have, I'm afraid, Nina, no more than a tiny income. You will either have to work – at what, I cannot imagine – or you will have to come and live with me. I think you must do the latter, anyway, because there is no question but that you need to sell this place; and what with property values falling, there is no certainty you will get a fair price for it, especially if you are too hasty to sell. Take time. And remember, you are very welcome at our house.'

I was happy and relieved to accept this offer. I liked Stephen's busy and attractive wife, Helena, who taught art and history at the grammar school in Cork, and wore outlandish hats and smoked. They were a calm and relaxing couple, childless, unfussy, clear-headed, and definite. They had a new villa at the end of the tree-lined walk of the Mardyke. It was small by comparison with the mansion at Cappoquin, but I loved its lightsomeness, its solid quality reflected in the oak block flooring with its diagonal shapes, the carved doorframes of elm, left untreated; the leaded panes of the windows. The garden had been laid out in the English cottage style, and I would spend the afternoons of the glorious summer of 1904 reading in the arbour made of teak, which carried a scent of Burma and the jungle when it was warmed by the sun. I grew more relaxed and became quieter in myself than I had been for years. My father was an addict, and he had the addict's tremulousness and scarcely contained anger about him all the time. He had been tired out from his vice and his pain, but I now realised that I had been exhausted by his continuously failing struggle with himself. Defeat is not only visited on the defeated; it spreads out to those on whom the victim has become dependent. I felt, sitting there in the garden on the Mardyke, no rancour whatever towards my father; but no regret either. I was sorry life had abused him, but then, he could have torn himself free from what had kept him captive. There can be, I think, no excuse for not freeing yourself from that which binds you. Many men, I fear, seek to entwine themselves ever more completely in the chains they once forged for themselves.

But not my Uncle Stephen. That new house, with its planted wisterias, its long narrow lawn, its tennis court smelling of cinders in the sunshine, the bathroom with the heavy iron bath and thick eau-de-nil tiles, all spoke of a fitness to the purpose — which was just to live in moderate comfort. I suppose he was what the communists would call a bourgeois, but if he was a bourgeois, then I liked it. I think I was as near as I've come to being carefree that summer, so when I met Morgan Holmes I was ready for romance, all the more so because of the slight tinge of danger surrounding him: he had something of a reputation. People spoke darkly of something hidden in his life, that his father had, once too often, to sweep things under the carpet.

He danced with me that night at the yacht club, and we walked outside onto the verandah overlooking the harbour. He continued to hold my hand, and I remember thinking, with approval, that his was dry in spite of the exertion of the dance. We stood then, cooling in the air, heavy with the smell of seaweed, and he asked me to a country house party being given by friends of his, the Kingstons, in Dunmanway. Over the next two days I walked in the garden in the summer heat, read, and would wander up and down the Mardyke under the dusty elms, the street deserted in the warmth. In those two days I fell in love with Morgan; or, it might be better to say, I allowed my feelings a little carnival, with Morgan as the centrepiece. We were married in six months, and we spent the New Year in Wiesbaden.

I don't think Morgan ever wanted children, although we did not take any precautions to prevent them coming. It just did not happen between us. Maybe it was me, but whenever I raised the subject with him, which was not often, he would brush it aside, propose an outing, or ask me inane questions about how I'd spent my day while he toiled (he used this word with irony) in the office. For years my life was stable, uneventful, in a kind of repose with, always, a little tremor of unease, a sparkling of tension. Breakfast with Morgan would sometimes be, for no reason I could ever discern, an agitated affair. I'd catch myself looking through the big panes of the morning-room windows, my mind straying forlornly over associations and vague disquiets: Father, his forehead against the windowpane, Morgan's stomach rumbling after sex as he dozed off. It used to seem as if my mind was the victim of whatever commotion stirred amongst its contents. But that was all. Nothing serious.

I used to think that all I needed was more activity, something to throw myself into, but I never mustered enough resolve. My days were a round of predictable events: coffee in Thompson's or the Tivoli in Patrick Street; an afternoon at bridge, or reading at home; then Morgan's return, dinner, bits and scraps of conversation; then bed with, possibly, sex. In this area Morgan was a bit of an enthusiast, always coming up with oddities and surprises. It meant hardly anything to me. I was aware of the urgency of his desire, but would observe him as from a height, like somebody watching from a clifftop a figure bent double amongst the rocks and sea wrack on the shoreline, picking mussels or limpets. He would be fiercely intent in that world while his fury would last, then quiet, a snooze, a stomach rumble. A not unpleasant routine, and one for which I am grateful, mildly.

Occasionally Uncle Stephen would call round, or I would visit him and Helena on the Mardyke. He seemed happy enough that I was not unhappy, and I knew from odd comments he'd make that to be in that condition, of temperate equanimity, was not, in his view, by any means to be despised.

They say you don't know a man until you live with him: I think a woman never knows a man, and vice versa. It's only those with enough romance in their nature to allow the luxury of illusion that maintain that any two people know each other, especially in marriage, where, if my own observation is anything to go by, people, on the whole, became strangers to each other, less intimate. There may be exceptions, but they are rare. What does come as a surprise is a swift change in behaviour, and that's what happened to Morgan some ten years or so ago.

I'd never seen him drunk, apart from that one wild occasion in Wiesbaden when he persuaded me – I have to admit I was not that hard to persuade – to do something dreadful with him in the cubicle of the communal swimming baths, with just the half-door blocking the view of our activities. There's no need to go into detail, but when I told him that we were being watched from the balcony by an old gentleman with a walrus moustache, who was grinning away like mad at me and winking (I was looking out; Morgan was busy with his back to the baths), this only increased his ardour, drunk and all as he was. But apart from that, he was a sober man, to my relief and comfort, bearing in mind the broken screams of my father as he clutched at his ruined stomach in his last agonies.

One night in 1919 or 1920 Morgan came home, much later than usual, about ten thirty. No phone call, which was entirely out of character. If a business acquaintance happened to arrive, and needed, say, to be entertained in the Cork and County Club, Morgan would always telephone. But that night, nothing. I sat in the drawing room, reading in the late summer light, then Morgan came in, completely drunk, scarcely able to stand. He sat opposite me in a heavy leather chair and started to talk. He went on non-stop for a half an hour, and as he did so I began to piece together, in astonishment, what he was telling me from his incoherent sallies of outrage and whines of complaint. I'd never seen him like this. My throat dried at the first sight of him, but as he maundered on I began to sweat in dismay.

He said that he'd come out at five as usual from the office. Condon was standing at the door ready to lock up, with that

Mull boy. He said goodnight and as he went outside a man
saunters across from where he was standing at the river wall,
and began to walk in step beside him. At first Morgan thought
he was a beggar, but when he didn't speak for a half a minute
or so, Morgan stopped and faced him, asking him what he
wanted. 'Nothing that you won't give when you know what
I know about you', was what this young man said; Morgan
repeated the phrase over and over. And he kept telling me that
the man had a coarse English accent. The young man, Owens
was his name, was under instructions, that's all he would say,
but he mentioned names – O'Dwyer, O'Dowd – and said that
all Morgan had to do was to look inside his mind and he'd
know why he was there, and what he had to do. When
Morgan asked him what that was, he was told the details didn't
matter, but that the time had come for Morgan to repay his
debt to life by doing something for the honour of his country.
I asked Morgan, in the deepening darkness, watching his ashen
face and fear-struck eyes why he didn't go straight to the RIC.
This was nothing more than a treasonable act, I said, meant to
upset people already upset enough in this distressed country.
And then he told me that he wasn't free to do that, out of
consideration for me. And then it dawned. Some scandal or
other had to be paid for. Face them down, I said; face them
down. But no. No good. They would stop at nothing, not
even execution.

He explained then, to me, in his own garbled way, that that
was how they worked. They, he said, were honest in admitting
they were no better than anyone else, but put above all else was
a dedication to something that meant nothing to the likes of us.
This made them merciless, and effective. Because they stood for
something. They knew, he said, that all human motive was
corrupt, but that didn't matter: it was the cause. Owens told
him that he, Owens, didn't matter to *Owens*; so how much less
did we matter to him. He could, Morgan told me, stand there
in that room and shoot us and not think about it. And then face
a firing squad with complete peace of mind. You can't face

them down, he said, because they will never give way. They know that we, accustomed to comfort and convenience, always will give way, because that is what has made us comfortable, our lives agreeable.

I swear if I had had a gun I would have shot Owens myself that moment. Owens had a hold over him, that was obvious. I tried, as best I could, to see if I could discover what that was. No. He was like a clam on that and I knew my life had changed for ever.

Within two weeks he was an alcoholic: emotional, talkative, self-pitying, full of contempt and self-contempt. And then, of course, the *coup de grâce*, the filth that he couldn't wait to discharge at me once his self-hate had begun to become his habitual state of mind. That he was the father of that Condon he'd taken on a year ago; that he'd done so at the mother's request; and that he'd say one thing for her, anyway, that *she* wasn't barren.

He complied with Owens's instructions, whatever they were. From what I could gather he was not required to do anything really dangerous. Financial support as required, and the storage of certain materials. I often wonder what my father would have said to an alcoholic son-in-law who is little better than a Fenian by virtue of what he does, with the added disgrace that his treason springs from no conviction, merely coercion based on fear. If I were Morgan Holmes, I think I'd prefer to be dead, which I think he himself feels at times.

My Uncle Stephen and Helena reacted to the change in our lives by leaving us almost entirely to ourselves, the way those marked down for disaster are avoided by an instinct wiser than logic. I could see this operating in Helena's face when I'd meet her in Grant's or Prince's Street as she bustled along, head down, woolly hat pulled over her ears.

1953

KATHERINE CONDON

There's a Polish boy has arrived next door. A refugee from the war. Mrs Falvey, the next door neighbour, has adopted him. He's called Stanley, his Polish name is Stanislaw. Mrs Falvey and her husband, James, have already one boy, a handsome child called Kevin, who has black hair and olive skin. The strange thing is that Kevin and Stanley could be brothers. I hear them over the wall at the back playing, Stanley babbling away in Polish and Kevin correcting him, gently. They are five and six years old, so that Kevin has had given to him, as if out of heaven, a brother. It's heartbreaking to see them walking out the long pathway to their front gate, arm in arm under the tall green flowering-currant hedge. I think sometimes that it's a pity any of us should grow up and become rough and hardened to life's crosses.

Sometimes the two little boys will stand at the metal gate, arms around each other's shoulders, looking at the passers-by. They spend a long time like that, or just exploring their garden these days, especially in the evening, now the days are getting longer. With my five, now, it's a different matter. The house is a bedlam, and I spend all my time trying to keep it clean and free of dust. That's the problem with older houses: dust every-where. I think the ideal family would be two, or maybe not even two: one, that you could devote all your attention to. Now I can hardly give any time to the eldest three with the twins newly arrived on the scene. Every time you get stuck it's a blow that knocks the joy out of life until eventually all you're left with is resignation to God's will, as the priest always says in confession. I never ask them their advice about anything because I know what they will say and even if they're right – and probably they are – it's still no consolation. How can I describe what they describe as 'the gift of children' does to you as they follow on, one after the other, and each time you pray for a miss? I know exactly what it feels like, but I can't put words on it. It has a colour, certainly, and that colour is grey. It's like this: you get them all off to school, and if Tim is on late shift you get him his breakfast; or if he's on nights you keep the kids quiet while they get ready for school. They're now trained enough to know if they make a noise, they get a clatter. God forgive me, but I get a thrill of satisfaction when I hit them. With them out of the way I go to Murphy's the butcher's, or Morrissey's for fish. Let's say it's Morrissey's for fish, and a Friday, or Wednesday in Lent. I always put my make-up on before I go out. I do this in front of the mirror in the hall, where I also take out my curlers. First I comb the hair, which is still thick and wiry, though its jet black is now going grey. I put on the rouge, then the lipstick, and run the pencil over my eyebrows, arching them as I do this. I'll hear Tim upstairs (if he's on nights) turning over in the bed, unable to sleep, sighing. And all the time I'm thinking: so this is life, this is it.

The lines are appearing around my eyes, and since my teeth were all taken out ('Get rid of them, Mrs Harding,' the dentist said, 'they're only a nuisance, and they're soft anyway from a poor diet in childhood') my upper lip has collapsed in on itself entirely, so that when I'm not talking it's a ridge of vertical wrinkles all across. How lucky Con is to be in the monastery at Melleray, out of all this. The hall is dark as I finish my make-up and light a cigarette before I go out. My consolation, better than the priest, or the company of Tim, or the children. I stand in the hallway, taking the odd look at myself in the mirror. I could take more of an interest, but I know where that leads to: Tim getting ideas, and the next thing you know is you're praying again for a deliverance from the routine of swelling, and awkwardness, and demands for sex (now that you're 'safe'), and eventual pains and shrieking. So it's better to let yourself go, although I can never bring myself to go out still in my curlers or without my lipstick, which some of them do even around here, which is quite a respectable address. And I always wash myself carefully and use deodorant. If the twins are sleeping, I'll take a chance and steal out without waking them: they'll be all right for a few minutes. Then the walk out to the gate, praying I won't meet Mrs Falvey, who's always too eager for a chat. Her husband, for all her dancing attendance on him, beats the tripe out of her when he's drunk: at least my fellow doesn't do that, or not too often anyway.

Mr Morrissey is a grey-haired man who brings the fish up from the market on fast days. He has a fat wife, who stands behind the counter of their big shop, arms folded, as she presides over her Mariettas, Lincoln Creams, turnips, potatoes, and cabbages. She always tries to carry an air of being better than the rest of us, and I suppose she is: she has the shop. You go through her domain if you need vegetables or tinned peas, or such like. The shelves are painted dirty white and covered with red-and-white checked paper, which hangs down over the lip of each one. They flutter slightly when you come in through the door that has a loud, even somewhat shocking, ping. I look at the tins of biscuits, racked and tilted in the dull light, and think how once their smell, when the glass lid would be opened, would set my teeth watering. Then you pass through into the cold smells of Mr Morrissey's fish shop.

His head is bent over a whiting or a mackerel, slicing into the gut. He holds the fish down with his left hand as he brings the knife along the white underbelly. Pushing, the guts splurge out, which he then detaches with a few strokes, wiping the bloody knife on his apron. His small body does not straighten as you tell him what you want. Right, Mrs Harding, a couple of nice whiting fillets. Then, he guts and beheads two he's held out to your gaze, and when the slices of flesh are cut free of bone and entrails, he dips them into an enamel basin filled with water brown from previous cleansings. He now slaps them down on the piled sheets of newspaper, where their wetness spreads a dark grey stain on the absorbent paper. Meanwhile, he dries his hands on his apron. Tucking the sides of the paper in first, he rolls the package towards you and when it is wrapped he hands you the pliant parcel. You think with dismay of what this will taste like. It will taste grey, like his hair, the gloomy shop, the kerbstones; it is the colour of the sighs that come down stairs when you turn the key on your way back in; it is the colour you are when one of the twins starts to cry.

I think I changed in some way when Ma died. Da had gone years before, in a smell of camphor and vomit. Cancer got him, in the private parts. They rotted away, I was told. All he could hope to hold in at the end was milk warmed by boiling water. And even that would come back up as often as not. I wept for him, and grieved: I remember howling with sorrow when Michael came down to tell me he was gone. I can also remember the eldest boy, Robert, looking at me in terror while I was crying, wondering what this was doing to me. How will he react when he hears of my death, or his father's?

But Ma's death was different. It was painless. One day she took a bad turn, went to Mrs Kenefick in the grocery shop to ring the doctor, and went to bed. The doctor came, examined her (she always felt she'd got her money's worth when she'd had an 'examination'), gave her some pills, and told her to stay in bed. This she did, which was not usual, because she never gave in to illness in her life, as far as I or anyone could remember. Michael called, as he did every day, letting himself in by the key on the string hanging from inside the door near the letterbox, and when he found she was not in the kitchen, as she always was, he called out. She replied from upstairs, and he went up, worried now. She was in her bed, her thin face above the bedclothes. She told him to call down to me, and then to get in contact with Con, and to tell the others. She said she was going, and told him just to get on with what she told him to do when he tried to say that she was going to be all right. 'I'm not all right and I don't mind', was what she said.

All of us gathered round the bed. There was Con, in his monk's habit, and me; and Michael and his wife Teresa. And there were the others as well: my sister Ann and her husband the lorry driver from Wexford, my brother Tom; Sarah in from the country. Fat Mag, now ancient and ailing, had come in from the country as well. We were all there. The Condons, and even one of the O'Dwyers, our close relatives over the years. Ma was breathing very lightly and her eyes were half shut, showing only the whites. Father Walsh, the parish priest, had been up to give her the last rites, and she had grown even more peaceful once the chrism had been put to her forehead and she had taken the host, which she did without too much difficulty.

With a great sigh, she opened her eyes, and called Michael over to her and whispered into his ear. He put his arms around her and raised her up on the bed, and she leaned back against the wooden headboard, eyes shut again. Then she spoke, very quietly, very deliberately. She said that we were all only lent to each other for a short time; that while we were here we didn't know one thing from another, good from bad, right from wrong. We should remember that whatever comes our way was not necessarily God's doing: that He was often too easily blamed by us for our own faults and shortcomings. That whatever happened to us was to be borne with patience, because any other course of action was a waste of time. Wishing for anything was no use; nor was prayer that was done with the aim of achieving or acquiring something. The only freedom we could any of us have was prayer made without any desire. Our troubles are never over while we draw breath. To be amongst other people is to be in trouble, which was why, she said, that family was so important, because bad and all as your own were, they were your own. She was glad to see us all together, and that we were all good to each other, because in the end, all that counted was family, because all other doings with people were full of danger. All we had to remember was our own uncharitable thoughts even towards the best of friends and we could see that friendship, love, affection, all those notions, were just dreams that you were wakened from at the first sign of trouble. The soft-hearted, she said, were never to be relied upon: they lived their lives in this dream, and they resented anyone who intruded into their own worlds. The soft-hearted had hard minds and selfish stomachs. They eat you up. Never love anyone other than God, she said, because all that was was foolishness.

She stopped then and sighed heavily once more, then her head dropped to one side. Her skin seemed to grow softer, and I saw, in her delicate, pointed chin, the frail line of her jaw, and her eyelids above the closed lashes gave a hint of what she would have been like as a girl, all those years ago. The blind rattled and I looked at it, yellow from age, a blank sheet in the colour and clutter of the room. It had the smell of the disinfectant that Ma used all over the house, but gradually this sharpness was being undercut by something else: an odour of sweetness, like the exhalation of daffodils that you get sometimes passing a large bunch of them in a vase in a dark hallway.

My husband Tim came in, just back from his late shift, so it would have been about fifteen minutes after midnight. She opened her eyes to see who it was; nodded at Tim and lifted her hand off the quilt. Then she died.

Tim and I were walking down the concrete steps between the iron railings, heading off home, when he said to me that it was a good thing that Con had got there just in time from Melleray. I asked him what he meant by that, seeing that Con had been there in plenty of time.

'My Jesus,' he said, 'you've put the fear of God into me.'

He stopped and held the round iron railing with one hand, and grabbed my arm with the other. I asked him what he meant.

'You won't believe this, but just as I was rounding Kenefick's corner there, I saw this man in a monk's habit walk up the road, come up these steps, stand at the door, knock, and be let in. I saw the light coming out onto the steps.'

I told him no one arrived before him.

'God between us and all harm,' Tim said.

All I know for me is that life is a mystery. I know that Ma is watching down on all of us, and I feel very ashamed when I think that she sees everything I do and knows everything that I think. She sees all my thoughts, and she knows how twisted they are. I hope she can find it in her to be patient with me, and with all of us. I think often, indeed most days, that I'd like to be with her among the dead, and along with all the Condons and O'Dwyers that have lived here for so many centuries. We are all alike, all sad and thoughtful, and full of rancour and feeling.

1964

TOM MULL

Everybody says what a wonderful summer it is. Wherever I go I'm made welcome. This is certainly one great town to take a vacation in. People are so friendly. My God, though, do they drink. I'm really quite happy to have so many drinking buddies at any hour of the day, because my days of toil are well and truly over. I'm in my seventies now, though I don't know for sure how old I am. My people never bothered about registering births or things like that. I assume I was baptised but where, I don't know, and I couldn't be bothered trying to find out. As if it matters. This is my first time back since I left in 1930, when Holmes started to get abusive: I told Condon then that he might take it, but not me, no sir, no way. Michael, God help him, was always too quiet for his own good. Maybe I should try to look him up? He could be dead. But I don't feel like doing much these days in Cork. I get up late in the Victoria, where I have a room overlooking Patrick Street. What a change: now all bright cars, and girls in short dresses standing outside Woolworth's or The Moderne across the road, licking ice creams, or jumping about with that restlessness kids have everywhere now. Then I take a bath, stroll down nice and easy for breakfast.

It's great the way they still keep the old ways going here – fine heavy cutlery, thick starched linen, napkins in pewter rings – so that when you wipe your mouth your lips are left completely clean and dry; and best of all, the big Irish breakfast which even has lamb chops and kidneys on offer if you want them. I always take whatever's going with the freshly squeezed orange juice that they do right there in the room with one of those old-fashioned glass things with the circle of spikes to stop the pith, and the rocket-shaped nose in the centre that looks for all the world like a nuclear warhead. Then I go off to buy a paper and take a walk.

The first walk I took was up Patrick Street and down Corn-market Street past the Bridewell. The market was in full swing with the stalls out in front of the shops selling everything that I remember from the old days: big heads of curly cabbage (to go with the bodice of ribs or pigs' heads or offal or streaky smoked bacon available from the butchers' shops across the way); working clothes; bedding that smelt of human use; chairs, tables, bedsteads, sprung mattresses; carpets; shoes piled in great heaps on handcarts. And all of this plenty of the used and the consumable being sold amidst the shouting and slagging of the women and men from their doorways or out in front of them, some with their hands filthy from scrabbling in the carrots, spuds, and turnips; others just standing with their shoulders up against the doorjambs, steady and easy, calling out their insults with the relaxed air of people who know where they belong.

I don't know how many times over in New York I'd think of this street with a dark and terrible longing. Sometimes I'd miss it so much, lying in my bed at night, especially in the early days, tired out after spending ten hours on my feet in a bar in the Bowery, that I'd actually start to cry, thinking of walking through the streets of a Saturday evening with my da, stopping for a pint – like that time with Holmes in the Old Weigh Bridge when Da sussed him out for a bastard – then heading up to home and the great smell of the cooking coming from the open turf fire. I'd be ashamed of myself then, and promise myself I'd not go on hankering like this but that I'd pull myself together and come back with the needful and show them all a thing or two. But no, it took me years to get myself into some kind of shape. I drank all the time, and was always broke in advance of payday. I drifted from one job to another, until I caught myself on, got married to this Swedish girl, a cook, and settled down. Then we started making money, but by that time Ma and Da were away, so there was nothing to bring me back home. I just put my shoulder to the wheel and started to make myself rich. Ellie Sørensen (that was her name) was Lutheran, and I got married in that Church (no problem: I'd not been to Mass nor meeting in years), her mom and dad beaming with pleasure.

They liked me from the start and were very satisfied that I'd agreed to marry in the Lutheran rite. I didn't say anything about how it was a matter of no importance to me. They helped a bit, at the start, with our first sandwich store, but now that I'd stopped drinking every day (I'd have a vodka or schnapps with Ellie on Sundays maybe) money seemed not to flow away from me any more: the opposite – it stuck. It is certainly true what they say in Cork, that the drunkard pisses his money away every night. Within a year we had a deli, then a liquor store, then two, then a bakery and so on. I don't know how much we're worth now, but my eldest son's a psychiatrist, my daughter a lawyer in Cincinnati, and the youngest boy is studying literature at Columbia. He's a bit weird: long hair and all that, but never mind.

Now I'm relaxed and my life's work is over I take a few drinks, and certainly this last week in Cork I've been drinking like I haven't done since those early years in the Bowery. I went into the Cornmarket Bar the first day here, at the end of the run of stalls and shops, and I don't think I've been in such a dump since I left the town over thirty years ago. It was mid-morning, and sunny, but the place was smelly, damp, and dark. The barman stood, his hands on the counter, a pint of stout in front of him, half of it gone. He drank the remainder off in two or three large swallows as I walked over to him. All the time he eyed me as the throat worked. He put the glass down with a thump.

'OK, Yank,' he said, 'what'll it be?'

'The same as yourself. Will you join me?'

Immediately the air changed. Briskness entered into his gesture. The glass was offered to the spout with a flourish, and the cream combed off the merging colours of black and brown and white with a spatula, which he flicked with elegance. I explained this was my first time back in my native city since I left as a fairly young man. By now a couple more had joined me at the counter, and I was buying drinks for them as well. I didn't mind. What the hell. Let them think I'm a fool and I'm loaded. I'm not a fool, but I am loaded, so what? I told them who I was, and that my ma and da had died, and that I'd lived up in Blarney Street, and that my father was Patrick Mull.

When I said that the barman said: 'Sure, Jesus, don't I remember him well. Many's the time I carried out the peelings to him my old ma used to keep under the sink. And he'd give you a balloon, or a bamboo whistle. You thought you were made-up, boy.'

My da had carried on his trade of inner-city pig rearing up to a few years before his death, and it turned out that all there in the bar could remember him well. They'd spoken to him, or as kids shouted abuse at him in the street. The glasses were empty, so I signalled to the barman, Mike Coveney (as it turned out he was the proprietor as well), to fill them up again.

'No way. No way,' he replied. 'We're all going to have a drink together to welcome you back to your native city. You are one of our own, Tom, and don't you forget. You're a Cork man, and, even more important than that, you're a Northsider.'

When his wife came in to help out at twelve o'clock nothing would do Coveney and his two cronies, Stevenson and Callaghan, but that they would come with me up to the old house on Blarney Street, although they warned me there'd been many changes. I couldn't believe my eyes: there were concrete flats now under construction at the turn off from Shandon Street, and when we got to where the house should have been, all that was left was the archway through into the courtyard. The courtyard itself was now paved with concrete, and the horses were gone. Breezeblock structures had been built, and from these units came various sounds: they were rented out to small-scale metalworkers, furniture-makers, and there was even a car-repair shop with an inspection pit. An access road had been made through the back yards of the houses above the site.

'This must be sad for you,' said Callaghan, a small thin man, with fine teeth and a nervous laugh and smile.

'No, no,' I said. 'The memories are still there. Progress is important. They're better off than we were.'

'They are to be sure,' said Coveney. 'Let's have one or two in the Old Reliable, then something to eat.'

Which we did. We came out of the Old Reliable, on Shandon Street, at ten in the evening, drunk but still solid, as Coveney said, and went into a fish and chip shop down the way. We walked back into the town centre, eating as we went, stopped for a while on the North Gate Bridge, and swore that this was, without doubt, the greatest city in the world. I was asked if I really believed that, now that I'd lived in New York for so many years. I swore that I did mean it, and at that moment it was all true. The night was alive in a way that I've never experienced in New York. In this city people live for the night. I remembered as a kid people saying to each other: 'What are you doing tonight?' Every day was spent planning the evening manoeuvres.

I've been back into Coveney's a few times since then, and each time it's almost impossible for me to buy a drink, or to buy anyone else one. And Stevenson, the other member of the trio that went up Blarney Street with me that first day, has asked me out to his house in Turner's Cross for lunch on Sunday.

'Come to Mass at twelve; we'll have a few pints in The Beer Garden and then we'll go up to our dinner.' Stevenson is a retired Guard, who came originally from the Cornmarket Street area (the Marsh, as we knew it) and goes back in there for his few daily pints. When I ring back home to Ellie, who is out holidaying in the Catskills with my son's in-laws, the Ratzenbergs, I tell her that this is a great town, that she'd love it (though I know she wouldn't) and that these people are independent, strong and confident. They are not like those I left, years ago.

I walk around all the time as if I can't take enough in. The kids I meet in the bars are curious about New York, and they kind of indulge me as the returned Yank. They have the arrogance of the young you find everywhere now. But why not? We were always too respectful. I walk around Paul Street, behind Patrick Street, and explore the new coffee bars there with trendy names, photographers' studios, art shops. Music thumps the air.

I don't know if I'll try to find Michael at all. I'm almost afraid to see what life has done to him. I think I prefer being anonymous here, meeting people casually in bars. I love the city, but want to be free of it too, somehow. It draws you in; best to keep a little distance from it. I ring Ellie: the weather is fine and clear, cool and freshening. I want to be back in New York, my true home, away from this city of memories and feelings. I saunter out the heavy glass doors of the Victoria, look over at the offices of the *Cork Examiner*. It's early, quarter to nine, and the girls are going to work all confident strides in their high heels and sheer stockings. I think I'm like my old da. I think I love life and all that happens in it. I'm like him climbing the hill up Shandon Street of an evening, head down, hand lightly engaged in the donkey's halter, smiling to myself, as the North Cathedral tolls out the bells for eight o'clock.

1640

GEOFFREY KEATING

The *History*, the *Groundwork*, is completed. It's over. I cannot
think how I can have managed this. The fear of my own
inability, incapacity; my presumption; my wilfulness; all these
now at an end, just me breathing. When I look at that thing
there on my writing table I do not know how or where I got
the energy to have faced into it. And what for? When will
what I have written assume the dignity of print? It is not
impossible that it never will, that the few copies made of that
thing by one of the O'Clerys from the north, a McEgan from
west of the Shannon, and one or two others, will be the extent
of its dissemination. For the glory of God? Hardly. That kind

of afflatus visits me very rarely now. There was a time when I could have conceived my labour as a divine injunction laid upon me as part of my responsibility to protect the faith and its truth on this island from the fomenting malefaction of usurpers and sodomites. But I've had enough of this kind of thing. And then I remember what it was like when I was a young priest in Bordeaux, fired up by faithful zeal, yes, but more than that, more than that. I remember (almost shameful to recall it now) weeping all night for seven nights in helpless grief when I heard the news of Mountjoy's shining victory at Kinsale. I saw it then all before me: the lies, the distortion, the compulsion to disgrace and the acceptance of it as a fated destiny, the enforced yielding that deludes itself by thinking it retains its liberty. All that. All that. I did not think that I would ever be able to stop that nightly caterwauling. It did stop, checked, probably, by what I have found is the only means of staying human hurt: writing. Or at least, those few embarrassing poems I wrote in Bordeaux seemed to install some facility for the deferral of grief. But never its erasure. Never. To this day, this very night as I look at the thick pile of folios, it rises within me, and I a foreigner, an Englishman, of all things. The dark reservoir of hurt and hate.

1955

ROBERT HARDING

Da was handy. He made two stools from butterboxes, one for each side of the fire. I remember they had writing on them. He painted them and hinged a lid on each, covering it with Dunlopillo foam, then upholstered that with Rexine stuff. Red it was, and the boxes, too, were painted a deep glossy red. My ma used to keep her knitting in them, and when Da would be on four to twelve, she'd sit there by the fire, knitting, all night. Or she'd read sometimes. She could read for hours upon end. 'Nothing like a good book,' she'd say to me. 'You're never on your own with a good book.' This was my ma, Katherine Condon.

She smoked a lot, and when she got upset her chest would heave in excitement, and I'd see her heart thumping against her breast. I could actually see her chest throb with her heartbeat. I think she was always lonely. Maybe because she loved people too much. This was my ma, Katherine Condon.

Funny name. She'd also sit on the butterbox when her friends would come in from Bishopstown or Ballyphehane, when they would laugh and laugh, shrieking at each other in mirth and holding their stomachs. The women would go wild with laughter, and they always laughed at the same thing: men. What they did, what they said, how they stood, how they walked, how they went to the toilet. They laughed at everything men did. This was the laughter of the women of Cork. And this is what I want to remember, as strongly as I can.

The laughter of the women of Cork. They never seemed to notice me amongst them. I was privileged, somehow, or maybe I was able to make myself unobtrusive. I don't know. They'd never allow any other children amongst them. Me, they overlooked. I'd sit under the table and would feel warm with delight in the middle of this mad, tearing, screaming laughter. It made everything all right. It removed all the terror of the playground and the anxiety of homework to hear these harsh ascents and descents of laughter. They'd stop and then one of them would start again and they'd all be off once more. My mother would cry tears of hilarity and plead with her sisters, or Mrs Barrett, or whomever, to stop for Jesus' sake. But they wouldn't. They'd laugh on and on until they'd hear the turn of the key as my da, that's Tim Harding, would come in from work, smelling of iron and metal and the night.